SO MANY TRUE BELIEVERS

SO MANY TRUE BELIEVERS

STORIES

TYRONE JAEGER

Queen's Ferry Press
8622 Naomi Street
Plano, TX 75024
www.queensferrypress.com

Thanks to the editors for publishing the following stories, though sometimes in different form and under different title:

"So Many True Believers" appeared in *The Oxford American*
"Liar's Lullaby" appeared in the anthology *Tartts Three: Incisive Writing from Emerging Writers* and originally in *Vanguard* (Australia)
"Legacy" appeared in *The Rio Grande Review*
"Mercy Comes Calling" appeared in *Southern Humanities Review* and won the 2012 Theodore Christian Hoepfner Award, given yearly to the best story in *SHR*
"These Are My Arms" appeared in *The Literary Review*
"Woe to You, Destroyer" appeared in *Eclipse*
"The Mermaid" appeared in *Beloit Fiction Journal*
"To Thy Speed Add Wings"apppeared in *descant* and winner of the 2014 Frank O'Connor Award for Short Fiction, given annually to the best short story in *descant*
"Ghost Image" appeared in *Portland Review*

Published 2016 by Queen's Ferry Press

Cover design by Brian Mihok

First edition February 2016

ISBN 978-1-938466-58-8

Printed in the United States of America

to Julee always

CONTENTS

SO MANY TRUE BELIEVERS

SOME NIGHTS, I DREAM OF MR. SPINOTELLI returning from the underwater cavern. In these dreams, he and I swim in the spring-fed depths. I try to speak to him through the water, but my throat constricts. Eventually, he glides away from me—back to the cave mouth. I wake from these dreams in a sweaty panic. In the hours it takes me to fall back to sleep, I am haunted by the words I attempt to say in the dream: *Tell me what you see. Tell me, is she out there?*

I should first tell you about Florida, five years before Estelle and I would part ways. We paddled on the Wekiva River. Morning fog blanketed the water and burned under the sun, sending up plumes like distress signals. Alligators, turtles, limpkins, and white ibis. The squawk of birds, the rattle of insects. Silently, the canoe cut the water, our paddling and breathing in tempo. Sunfish darted around us, a gray heron waded knee-deep near shore. I sat behind Estelle and—it's only now, so many years later, that I see it—in the ashen fog she looked like she was piloting the canoe between two worlds.

We switched places. She rowed, and I faced her, holding a photocopied script of the musical *Anchors Aweigh*. Estelle practiced her part—the lead role of an aspiring singer with big-screen ambitions—and though she still stumbled over her lines, she sang with perfect abandon. *All of the sudden, my heart sings, when I remember little things...*

After we reached the shore, we spread a blanket on the bank of the springs and baked in the sun. Estelle said, "I feel the presence of entities and energies." In the sixteen months that I had known Estelle, I tried to sense the things she often mentioned, but I failed.

The reflections of evergreens, cypress, and hyacinth purled in the water. "Belief can transform the humdrum into the fantastic," she said. She memorized such maxims from self-help books as if she was still trying to convince herself.

"Your singing was fantastic," I said. I lay down and, looking up at the sky, placed my hands together in mock prayer. "May I have your autograph?" She traced her name in the sweat beaded on my belly.

We dove near the mouth of the cavern—where the water boiled—but the currents pushed us back. The cave was reputed to be hundreds of feet deep, but its entrance was too narrow to ever tempt us inside. Years later, after several tragic incidents, they would cap the entrance with steel bars to prevent thrill-seekers from exploration. That day, as we swam, Estelle's laughter echoed across the water. "Jeremy," she said, "let's play Mother, Circa 1965." This was the game we had devised in homage to my mother's former career.

When my mother was eighteen, she flew from Nebraska to Florida and ended up performing as a mermaid at Weeki Wachee Springs. There she met my father, who still tells his love-at-first-sight story: she, a mermaid dancing underwater, and he, an English professor watching through the glass, transfixed. "I met a true siren," my father will say, "and ever since—in accordance with the legends—she's been trying to drown me." My mother was no longer a mermaid, but she was old friends with the director of *Anchors Aweigh* and had exerted some influence for Estelle's sake.

In the water, Estelle and I faced each other, held hands, and chanted, "Mother, Circa 1965!" before sinking to the bottom. Estelle blew out air, made a funny expression. I tried to remain calm and focused, but when pressure developed in my chest and head, I pushed upward, breaking the surface. Below, Estelle turned and swam away. When we played Mother, Circa 1965, she always won.

She finally came up for air, hair plastered to her face. She said, "Believe!" and then released her singsong laughter.

I wasn't sure if the command was meant for me or if it was a self-affirmation lifted from one of her books.

I flipped on my back and kicked until I touched her hands. She was tan, her body fit from yoga and rollerblading. I held her tight and we slid under the surface and kissed. Her teeth were white stones beneath the water.

At sunset of the same day, I pushed a lawn mower across the blind and elderly Mr. Spinotelli's yard. In a lace-curtained window, a pink neon sign glowed: *PSYCHIC*. Every time I mowed for Mr. Spinotelli, he read Estelle's cards; they spoke the same language, words I could not understand, the Esperanto of a sixth sense. His tarot deck, I knew, was freckled with Braille. I was stoned on Valium. Beneath my feet, the damp and spongy grass felt like the terrain of a dream. I was one year out of college and had my first real job—a teacher at a high school of last resort. Estelle and I were saving money, so we both waited tables. I also kept some of the lawn gigs I had worked during college. Many of the senior citizens I worked for stored pills in their medicine cabinets—my sole employee benefit—but Mr. Spinotelli's cabinet held nothing save for Tiger Balm and Crystal deodorant.

When I finished cutting the grass, I loaded the mower onto my pickup truck. Estelle—in a tight white T-shirt, wrap skirt, and flip-flops—walked out the front door. She said, "Mr. Spinotelli says that he's received his boarding pass." A jet roared in the orange sky and Estelle pointed. "Look! The vapor trail is like the tail of a comet."

Estelle got in the truck's passenger seat, fanning herself with the *Anchors Aweigh* script. She stuck her head out the window, her face at once shocked and gleeful. "He's heaven-bound. They contacted him. He's marked May 15, 1992 on his calendar. One month from now."

"You're beautiful when you're making no sense," I said.

She avoided my gaze. "They're aliens. Laugh. I know you want to." Estelle was the kind of young woman prone to melancholy, and I saw it rising in the slow and cautious movements of her eyes. I had met her at a chain Italian restaurant where she worked full-time and I picked up the occasional shift. During our first shift together, she had told me about reading Whitley Strieber's abduction memoir, *Communion: A True Story.* "Imagine what I thought," she had said, "when I realized that aliens were here among us." Within six months, we had moved in together. During our first week of cohabitation, a psychic told Estelle: "Problems will arise with an unbeliever." Sure enough, that night we argued over predictions and self-fulfilling prophecies. We hadn't even had time to unpack. Her belief drove me mad and into fits of jealousy—and yet it also excited me.

We heard the front door close. Mr. Spinotelli stood on the steps. "The lawn smells terrific," he said.

"But it looks like hell," I said.

"No matter. I'll fix it up after you leave."

This was our running joke. Mr. Spinotelli had lost his sight as a teenager, but he claimed to have done all his own mowing until his knees gave him too much pain—that's why he hired me.

"In 1957," Mr. Spinotelli said, "many years after I had lost my sight, I reshingled the bungalow's roof at nighttime. The neighbors caused a fuss, but what does darkness mean to a blind man?"

I reached for the money in his hand. He grabbed my fingertips, squeezing until I winced. "She told you, didn't she?" he said. Air conditioning hummed, and though I hadn't been inside his house in a while, I knew that white candles burned and homemade potpourri simmered in small crocks. His clouded gaze made me feel exposed, as if he detected something in me. I pulled my fingers from his grasp, the twenty-dollar bill now mine. The old man shuffled to the truck and touched Estelle's arm. "They'll be coming to harvest me soon," he said, before turning back to his house.

I climbed into the truck. "I'm having the sensation that for the first time my eyes are *really* open," Estelle said. She put her bare feet up on the dash—it was a pose that she knew I found irresistible.

"This isn't the first time, Estelle," I said. "You're bullshitting me." She scraped at the red nail polish on her big toenail and flicked some at me.

"But wouldn't it be wonderful?" she said. "Imagine—he goes somewhere faraway and exotic, more beautiful than our river, a place we couldn't even dream up."

"He's dreamed it up all right."

"It's perfectly harmless," she said. "Love and kindness are central to his beliefs."

We each lit a cigarette. I put the truck in gear and we drove Orlando's streets, making our way back home. She blew smoke around my head. We passed the sinkhole that had swallowed the Krishna temple, an Ethiopian restaurant that was once a Long John Silver's, and an office park that sat on former wetlands. Estelle put her feet in my lap and worked me toward complete distraction.

"My problem," I said, "is that I don't know how much of this you buy."

She placed her foot against my cheek. "He said that we'll get married but not until we're old."

"We?" I said.

"Me and you, silly. He said that someday I'll touch the hand of the Dalai Lama, probably in St. Louis. And he said that fame awaits me." I asked what she would do if she could choose only one. "I *don't* have to make that choice," she said.

—

For the next month, Estelle and I lived in the frenzy of *Anchors Aweigh* rehearsals. During my childhood, I had become familiar with my mother's acting routine—the panic of rehearsals, the rush of performances, and the lull between shows. Estelle worked lunch shifts at the restaurant, rehearsed until late into the night, and in her rare free time, she visited Mr. Spinotelli. He read her fortune and they discussed past lives, crystals, spiritual evolution, and the fashion sense of extraterrestrials.

Estelle and I thought that if things went well with the musical, we would move to Los Angeles or New York.

A touring company had invited her to audition after *Anchors Aweigh* closed. Though the job, if she got it, would keep her on the road eleven months of the year, they promised that she would be able to visit home several times. To me, it seemed like no kind of life. She and I bickered about her career. Mr. Spinotelli told her that I was a *pool of negative energy*, and we fought about this, too.

Each and every day at the school of last resort, I was tested: the students, whether they cared or not, were a population marked to be saved or discarded. I lost more battles than I won. I picked up weekend shifts at the restaurant, and there I flirted with a blonde cashier who thought I was funny, and when she gave me change, our fingers touched—lingered—in a way that predicted chaos. At night, I slept less and less. In bed, I listened to Coast-to-Coast AM on the radio, where the talk centered on UFOs and supernatural conspiracies. Whitley Strieber was a frequent guest, and, with no irony whatsoever, he spoke of his abductions. By listening, I hoped to understand Estelle's fascination with Mr. Spinotelli. Instead, I now met aliens and ghosts in my nightmares.

The day before the opening night of *Anchors Aweigh*, I mowed Spinotelli's yard while Estelle sat inside for a reading, one just for the show. I ran the mower back and forth by the dining-room window and, inside, the old man and Estelle sat at his table. Estelle leaned across the tarot deck and placed her hands on Spinotelli's face, tracing the curve of his whiskered jaw and his hairline. She knelt beside him, lifting his hands from the table and placing his fingers on her eyes and cheeks. After she took her seat again, she nodded as he spoke. I switched off the mower. They both faced the window. I waved but they sat unmoving, so I yanked the pull cord, igniting an ugly wall of sound.

After Spinotelli paid me, I said, "What's the forecast, rain or shine?"

"She'll do splendidly," he said.

"So you sensed splendid by touching her face?"

He was quiet for a moment. "Your thoughts lack dimension," he said.

"Am I supposed to understand what that means?"

"Rather than evolve, you'll be stranded on an island of your own foolishness. You'll drown in ignorance."

Sweat dripped down my ribcage. I may not have said a word. I may have said, "Okay, mister spaceman." I honestly don't remember.

Opening night of *Anchors Aweigh*, my parents and I sat in the second row. In a pencil skirt and a blouse with a scooped neckline, Estelle, as Susan Abbott—who drives two sailors into a frenzy of admiration—said, "Now, listen...no matter what happens, be brave." She sang a blue tango called "Jealousy." Every time I saw Estelle perform on stage—whether in a play or musical, or even at karaoke—my heart filled with a generosity that I could not sustain.

In the lobby during intermission, my father said, "That Estelle, she's stealing the show." My mother pulled us in close and said, "This role is perfect for her. She's always been a better singer than an actress." During the second act, Estelle crooned "All of the Sudden My Heart Sings," each note pulling her higher on some invisible cable until it seemed she was singing from the rafters.

My parents came to the closing show, too. After final curtain, and in preparation for the cast party, I popped a few Valium, compliments of the Widow Haberstadt, another lawn client. With the exception of my mother and Estelle, talented people made me nervous, and theater parties were a special kind of torture. I chatted with my parents. My mother, a petite woman in a pink dress, evaluated the talent in the room. My father, hair VO5'ed back from his forehead, left frequently to refill our martini glasses.

It was a typical cast party—everyone laughing with their mouths too wide, as if projecting to a vast audience. Estelle wore a rose in her hair and when she saw us she waved, looking relieved. My father planted a kiss on her forehead. "Straight to the top, kiddo," he said.

"If I could sing like you," my mother said, "I could have performed on land rather than underwater."

"We know better than that," Estelle said. "I want to thank you again." She kissed my mother's powdered cheek, pulled the rose from her hair, and presented it to my mother.

My mother shrugged and sniffed the rose. "It's your talent, dear. I simply brought it to the attention of the right people."

Estelle said she'd had it on good authority that the run would go so well. My parents were confused about who that authority might be, and Estelle laughed as they went down a list of critics, actors, and directors. "Him?" My father jerked his thumb at me.

"No, not me," I said. "She means Mr. Spinotelli. The blind lunatic who thinks space people are coming to harvest his body."

In the corner, a group of actors dressed as sailors had taken off their shirts and were drawing pen-and-ink tattoos on one another. "They're not exactly space *people*," Estelle said.

"Does he do astrology charts?" my mother said. "I had mine done a few years ago and for the life of me I can't find it."

"I stand corrected," I said. "Space *aliens* are going to land and recycle his body."

"You're drunk," my father said to me.

"Does an astrology chart expire?" my mother said.

"Her psychic is into some deep-space ecology," I said.

"We all love trees, honey," my mother said, "but I want to know if my chart needs to be updated." The sailors frolicked and made muscles. Wet tattoos of naked men danced on their arms.

"Mr. Spinotelli is engaged in cutting-edge symbology," Estelle said. She touched my father's elbow. "It's a system that utilizes technology, the Bible, and certain divination techniques that contemporary thinkers have intentionally neglected."

I had never heard her speak like this before.

"Let it be new!" my father said. "Forget the old religions and on with the new millennialism." He finished off his martini. He was typically a serious individual, but Estelle's presence always turned him into an overgrown and overeducated child. "In the best utopian fiction, aliens practice the most sophisticated forms of socialism."

"Dear, you didn't put my astrology chart away with the Triple-A maps, did you?"

"Personally," Estelle said, "I don't see a qualitative difference between old religions and new. Name a so-called religion that wasn't once a cult."

"My point exactly," my father said.

"Your father has never approved, but I still claim Catholicism as my religion," my mother said.

"Jeremy's a skeptic," Estelle said.

"Just because I don't believe in Martians, like you—"

"Are you trying to tell a story," Estelle said, "or are you just trying to embarrass me?"

"I hate to say it," my father said, "but I may have let the Triple-A membership expire."

"He's a clown, Estelle, a fraud."

The sailors in the corner had formed a human pyramid and were singing "Ninety-Nine Bottles of Beer."

"I've always thought," my mother said, "that the Egyptians were a forward-looking people."

"Besides your present inebriation," Estelle said to me, "your problem is a general distrust of the people who love you. It's easier to not believe than to trust."

My mother played with her hair. My father chewed on his olive, dislodged the pimento, and spat it back into his glass. "Jeremy's always been incorrigible that way," he said.

I reached for words that bobbed and swayed behind the drinks and the painkillers. "I worry is all," I finally said. My parents and Estelle shared looks of equal parts worry and fear. I raised my glass. "Here's to the spaceman," I said. I put my free hand on Estelle's shoulder. She removed my hand and secured it around my martini glass. "You need two hands," she said.

The drunken sailors called her name and demanded a song. She belted out the title track: *Anchors aweigh, my boys, anchors aweigh... Until we meet once more, here's wishing you a happy voyage home!* She received a round of applause. I joined in, dropping my drink. Broken glass shattered at my feet, but with the applause and cheering, no one noticed.

A few weeks later, in mid-May, Mr. Spinotelli, Estelle, and I paddled the Wekiva River. Estelle had suggested the trip as a kind of peace offering for us. She sat bow and I sat stern, and we leaned over the sides of the boat, prodding the lily pads with our paddles. Mr. Spinotelli sat in the hull, his hand trailing in the water, and he asked me to describe what I saw.

I told him how in the distance the whiteness of great egrets spotted the dense green foliage of a live oak. Three vultures perched high on the dead branches of a cypress. Turtles sunbathed on a fallen limb arcing out of the water and, below us, sunfish turned in the current as if their mission continually changed.

Mr. Spinotelli stood, his hands out for balance, his damaged knees shaky. "Stop the boat!" he shouted. Inhaling deeply, making an ostentatious display, he launched into "All of the Sudden My Heart Sings." I considered pushing him into the river. He was a terrible singer, but I found myself chuckling and then singing along. My laughter was generous for once. When Estelle joined in, I reached for her hand.

We paddled to the springs. It was a Friday, early evening, the sky seeming to explode in deep colors. Shadows hatched across the swimming hole and mothers called to their children. Sunbathers began packing away their towels, books, and blankets. The cicadas buzzed and the smell of grilled chicken hung in the air.

We slipped into the water. "Let's play Mother, Circa 1965," Estelle said. Mr. Spinotelli laughed at the very name. Surprisingly enough, he was a strong swimmer, but I doubted he had much practice holding his breath. Estelle whispered in my ear: "We'll close our eyes. It's only fair."

We said, "Mother Circa 1965," and I had never heard so much happiness in Mr. Spinotelli's voice. As I went under, it seemed that the injuries we had each caused had been forgiven. Underwater, time vanished. I opened my eyes to see Estelle swimming toward Mr. Spinotelli, who was headed for the cave, his legs kicking powerfully against the current. Twisting his body, he entered the dark opening and vanished.

I broke to the surface, choking and gasping. Estelle was still below, swimming in place, alone, no sign of Spinotelli.

Then she was next to me. I said, "Where does he think he's going?" She studied my face, as if to say *Where do you think?*

I knew the springs were swim-at-your-own-risk, so I started yelling: "He's gone down in the cave! He's blind!" I dove down and swam toward the opening. The light played upon the green of the water, the white of the rocks...nothing but darkness beyond. When my arms began to hurt, I swam back up.

"He said not to be afraid," Estelle said. "He wanted us here as witnesses."

I understood that she suspected we'd never recover Spinotelli. The next few hours passed in a confused rush. The sunset was spectacular, the lower atmosphere charged with hues of gold and rose. A crowd gathered and would-be heroes dove down, but, like me, came up panting. We stood by the water, Estelle at my side. Even in my state of panic, I recognized that her skin radiated a luminosity that makeup and stage lighting could never reproduce.

A ranger arrived and cleared the water. We explained that Spinotelli was blind and that he had somehow swum into the mouth of the cavern and disappeared. Someone laughed, and Estelle said, "I don't think you'll find him." The ranger put his finger on my chest. "This best not be a joke."

A man said, "I saw these two in a canoe with an old man, and he was singing at the top of his lungs."

Estelle pointed up above the cypress. "A comet," she said. We all turned to look, but I saw nothing but the night's first star. Someone said, "Make a wish." The police, the divers, and the spotlights arrived. Local TV vans pulled into the parking lot. Reluctant scuba divers with flashlights in hand submerged themselves.

Estelle faced the television cameras. "He swam into the cave, yes," she said, her voice tinged with the airy intonations of a witness to a miracle. "Such departures have been recorded throughout human history."

The TV guys shared a look, and the interview soon ended. One whispered to me, "Bub, I think she's in shock."

Still in our bathing suits, Estelle and I stood huddled under a blanket, our hair wet. Somewhere we had clothes, but I couldn't remember where.

I said, "He's dead."

"You're in denial," she said.

"Don't do this," I said.

The sky was midnight, and she looked up as if she expected the blue to part like a curtain for some Great Benign to descend upon us. It made little sense—did she think the cavern was the concourse to some mother ship?—and even as we stood with our skin touching, when the moment was right to say, *My God, Estelle, I'm sorry,* I instead said, "If you're so convinced, why didn't you follow?"

"I already have," she said. Had the cameras recorded this moment, I'm sure our faces would have appeared as innocent as those of all liars convinced of their stories.

We didn't sleep that night. We brought the TV into the bedroom. We watched the news, and the story ran without a single quote from Estelle. "They don't want the truth," she said. With a pile of pills and an ashtray between us, we flipped through channels the entire night, stopping to watch the last five minutes of a Jacques Cousteau documentary, an episode of *Cosmos,* and then hours of psychic hotlines. At some point, I stopped watching and traced a finger down Estelle's ribs and then up her hip. She looked at my hand, whispered my name, as if to say, *We've parted,* and I removed my hand. I fell asleep numb, and I imagine Estelle did the same.

After Mr. Spinotelli's death, Estelle drove to Wilmington, North Carolina, and auditioned for the touring company, and I slept with the blonde from the restaurant. The sex—the one time we ever slept together—was slow and full of sorrow. The blonde and I had become close friends, and in an easier world we might have married. The touring company hired Estelle—she accepted— and two weeks later, on my convincing, she quit. We never returned to the springs. We never followed up on the Los Angeles or New York plans. We stayed in a holding pattern, uncertain where we would land.

My love for Estelle had been corrupted by the knowledge that she would leave, but the evening that Hurricane Andrew hit, I was the one who packed a suitcase.

"I know about *her,*" Estelle said. "I knew the entire time." We both pretended the blonde cashier had caused our split.

Estelle moved to New York. She spoke her monologues and sang her songs to people who never called her back. I relocated to Colorado. My mother told me that she had seen Estelle on late-night television. "I don't know who the costume designers were," she said, "but Estelle had this awful short haircut and wore a man's shirt. It was all very *Star Trek* meets Sunday school."

Estelle occasionally wrote me letters. In one of the last, she wrote: "I touched the hand of the Dalai Lama, and you're not going to believe in what city!"

A few years later, in the spring of 1997, I was headed to Orlando from Denver, where I was again teaching miscreants, this time at a place called the Nat Mota School. On the moving sidewalk, at the Denver airport, six women shuttled past me. They had crew cuts and wore baggy shirts buttoned at the collar. They were giggling and pointing out the windows at the terminal's unusual roof cones.

I recognized her laugh before I saw her. I said her name and two of the women turned and looked at me suspiciously. They closed ranks around her and began to walk faster. She lifted her chin, apparently making a point to not look my way. I shouted her name again. Off the moving sidewalk, they hustled to the restroom. I caught up and waited outside, feeling like a creep, but wondering why she would ignore me. Within seconds, Estelle walked out alone. "Quick," she whispered. I followed her to the concourse trains, where we stood and waited for the next to arrive.

"What's going on?" I said.

She smiled and though too thin and in ugly clothes, she was still undeniably attractive. "I like the pixie hair," I said. "But what's the deal with your friends?" Over the PA system, a woman's voice said, *The train is arriving.* Estelle grabbed my sleeve and pulled me onto the train, where we sat on the front bench.

"The Automated Guideway Transit System," she said. "I love it! How does one get a job naming transport?" I shrugged my shoulders and waited for her to verbally acknowledge our chance meeting.

"Estelle?"

"Call me Estody," she said. "My name is now Estody." The chimes sounded again and travelers hurried through the sliding silver doors. *The doors are closing,* the automated voice said.

"Those women are my classmates," she said. "You look scared." Her saying it made it so.

It had been five years since we had been face-to-face. "My parents still ask about you," I said. "My mother saw you on TV."

"I've met the most wonderful people," she said.

"The Dalai Lama?" I said.

"More importantly, I've met my spiritual guide."

"I moved in with a nursing student in Denver. Things aren't good."

Her eyes searched mine. During my years of teaching, I had learned to listen—or rather, to stay quiet and let words wash over me. She told me she was living down in San Diego in a collective. With some of her classmates, as she called them, she had splurged on tickets to Denver. They were here to visit the recently opened airport, which they believed was awash in holy messages. Their return flight would leave for San Diego in an hour. "We're allowing ourselves a huge material vacation before we enter the next level of our studies. The airport was my idea."

"I'm on my way to visit home. Florida." I didn't know what else to say.

"I need to get back. Those classmates of mine are a nervous bunch. They've probably put out an APB already." The train riders gripped ceiling handles, they leaned on chrome poles, and they stared at Estelle. She gently laid her hand over mine, a graceful yet condescending gesture. "As members of The Transition classroom, we avoid physical contact. We don't even hug."

"What have you gotten yourself into?" I said.

"Don't say it like that."

25

Always a coward, I said, "Do you need anything?"

"We have a vehicle that will be waiting for us," she said. "It's behind Hale-Bopp. Can you believe that?" She stood and then sat back down. "Since you asked," she said. "There is one thing. We'll be leaving. We all go willingly, but in the media they'll say awful things, like we had bad relationships with our parents, that we were vulnerable and easily brainwashed." She wiped her eyes. "How could I turn down the opportunity to advance to the next level?"

The automated voice said, *You are approaching the exit for all A gates.* I picked up my backpack. "My flight," I said.

We stepped off the train and her five classmates stood waiting at the foot of the escalator. Estelle's smile faded, fixed into some finality that I didn't want to believe. She leaned in and, with what I imagine as defiance, hugged me. She kissed my cheek.

My skin prickled. I wanted to say something. But I stood there feeling awkward and ill-prepared.

Less than a week later, I was watching television in my parents' living room when the news broke. The Hale-Bopp comet had passed behind Jupiter and the dead were discovered on their beds and bunks, Nike shoes, black pants, and purple shrouds covering them. Phenobarbital in their blood. Plastic bags on their heads. They believed that a spaceship, their mother ship, flew behind the comet. An old man with earnest eyes was their leader, and he had taught them that they would soon rise to the Evolutionary Level Above Human. Of course, they needed to die before they evolved. The coverage was non-stop.

I called the school in Denver and told them that I had a family emergency. The week following the suicides, a TV news report chronicled their last days, their travels and spending sprees, their last supper of turkey potpies and cheesecake with blueberries. With my parents, I watched clips of their "Earth Exit" videos, where the members said goodbye. Two of the women I recognized as Estelle's classmates from the airport.

Estelle's video was shown last—at twenty-eight, she was the youngest. When she identified herself as Estody, my mother said, "What a horrible name for such a beautiful girl."

My father said, "Will someone please tell me if any of this is real?"

In her videotape, Estelle is seated in front of tall trees. Birds sing throughout her monologue, a speech which I am now certain was practiced on me in the tunnels of the Denver airport.

In the tape's concluding moments, she pauses. She looks away from the camera, stage right, before looking back into the lens and straight into my eyes. She says, "Ta-da!" and laughs, singsong as usual. "Cut! Is that a wrap?" she says.

Sometimes when I wake from the dreams of swimming with Mr. Spinotelli, I expect to find Estelle next to me. Her hand on my face, her dark hair hanging down, she says, "You were having a bad dream, sweet boy," and she bursts into a song that sends the birds flying from the trees and the turtles diving into the water. On occasion, I too must comfort myself with a lie.

LIAR'S LULLABY

FROM YOUR POSITION NEXT TO THE BRIDE up on the steps of the bandshell, you notice Jeremy, in the back row of seating, trying to catch your eye. He looks good in a moss-green suit, though you wish that you hadn't invited him to the wedding so early during that first date. You make a rule: never make a second date before the first one is over. You smile back, only because you like the way it hurts to smile when you're crying. But it's a smile controlled by the zygomatic muscle, not a real smile, which also includes the orbicularis oculi that surround the eyes.

When Darla says "I will" to Quinn, you again feel your face swell with tears. You're a nursing student, and you ate three bananas for breakfast. Bananas contain tryptophan, an amino acid that the body synthesizes into serotonin, which regulates the emotions. Sometimes you think you should study nutrition instead.

After the ceremony, you search through the contents of your blue-striped canvas purse—elastic strip, cigarette lighter, plastic-sealed hypodermic, various cosmetics, gutted lipstick case containing baggy with crushed morphine tablets, cotton balls, two condoms, pack of cigarettes, and tissues. You consider the nature of love, its relationship with death, and pull out more tissues. Across town is the funeral of a former patient.

Darla and Quinn embrace equality so there is no special table up front for the wedding party. The wedding guests at your table smoke with cinematic abandon, as if they know how good cigarettes look on film. You light one yourself, which gets you a quick look from the only non-puffer at the table, an older white-haired woman. Smoking is an ongoing battle—quitting, longing, starting again. You had a smoking relapse when you recommenced getting high. Falling off the wagon has always given you terrible pleasure.

"It's a filthy habit," you say. "The irony is that I study health." You want to tell her how nicotine speeds up the heart, how the nervous system adjusts the vagus nerve, slowing down the heart and restoring equilibrium, but you keep it to yourself.

You exchange introductions with Desiree Maxime, who looks aristocratic with her white pageboy cut. Desiree purses her deep red lips (orbicularis oris) and then forms a smile (orbicularis oculi and zygomatic). "I like a cigarette now and again," she says. You open your pack for her, deciding that you will be good friends.

"Do you know my nephew, Ryan?" Desiree says.

In fact, you do. In high school, you used to buy prescription painkillers from Ryan. Knowing that he sometimes lived with his aunt, you wonder if he stole the pills from Desiree.

Ryan salutes you from across the table. He is friends with your date and with your brother—Shane—the wedding photographer, who now sits down next to you and Jeremy. Darla told you that she chose Shane to be the photographer because she once read a short story called "The Bride's Lover" in which a woman hires her ex-lover to document her wedding. You reminded her that they were never really *lovers* in a strict sense, and she agreed and then footnoted her agreement, adding that they had indeed once or twice *loved*, inserting the finger of one hand into the fist of the other.

Whatever, you thought. It is what it is, right? Now, your best friend is getting married to another old friend. Still, you've noticed the way that the bride and your brother occasionally lock eyes. You'd die for a look like that.

You introduce Desiree to Shane but not to Jeremy. Jeremy grabs Shane's shoulder and says, "Shane is one of my oldest and dearest friends. I grew up in Florida. That's where I know both of them from, from when they would visit their dad, who was a neighbor."

"He and I weren't really friends," you say to Desiree.

"We're on our second date," Jeremy explains to Desiree. Shane looks bored and searches the crowd for the wedding couple.

"This is a beautiful day for a wedding," Jeremy says.

"Doesn't he look like Brian Jones?" you say to Desiree.

"The dead Rolling Stone?" she says.

"Are you wishing me ill fortune?" Jeremy says.

"It's a morality tale," Shane says, taking Jeremy's picture and then yours.

"I love weddings," Jeremy says.

Last week, on your date—drinks at a your local bar—you told Jeremy about your list of overplayed-but-still-awesome wedding songs, which included "YMCA," your favorite. He said that he could only dance to live music. A friend from the hospital, Julius, an orderly with whom you've been intimate but never involved, sat down on a barstool next to yours. The band took the small stage and for few a minutes—who was counting?—you talked with Julius. When you turned back to Jeremy, he began drinking at an alarming rate. He babbled on about an ex-girlfriend—an actress—and UFOs and how he needed to escape Florida after the breakup. After an hour of this, you suggested another bar, hoping the change of atmosphere might sway the conversation in another direction. On the way, he jokingly-but-not-jokingly suggested that you give him a blowjob in an alleyway. When you entered the second bar, you excused yourself to use the ladies' room, exited through the back door and hailed a cab.

When you explained the failed date to Darla, she said that maybe Jeremy was jealous of Julius, hence embarrassed, but still attracted to you. She reminded you that you had RSVP-ed *guest plus one*, and if you couldn't find another plus one, you might as well bring Jeremy. Besides, she had said, if he turns out to be a complete dolt, dump him on your brother.

"Are you Irish?" Desiree says. "Those blue eyes have to be your best feature," she says.

"Thank you," you say. "I am."

"Beautiful skin, too," she says.

"I love her hair," Jeremy says. Everyone at the table nods and smiles. You don't react. He says, "That hair. Those pigtails! It's like rusty wires coursing with electricity."

"Thanks, Jeremy," you say, feeling reluctantly flattered. You refuse to touch your hair, although now your pigtails seem to tingle. "A girl can't be too shocking," you say. Maybe you've short-circuited, and maybe he drinks to self-medicate an anxiety disorder. You consider forgiving him.

In the last two years, five of your best friends have married. If you ever marry, you'd prefer to elope. You like the word *elope*, the way it sounds foreign and rhymes with *antelope*, which sounds like *antidote*.

Darla is one of your best friends and one of the few who know about "Colleen's Little Secret." Five days ago, she joked that her wedding was an intravenous drug-free zone. Trying not to sound offended, you told her that you hadn't been using. Trying not to offend, she avoided looking at the long sleeves you were wearing in ninety-degree weather.

At the hospital, Julius showed you his locker, which contains a collection of sticky notes, each inked with the name of a patient whose death he has witnessed. When your face went pale, he said, "You look like you need a corrective." From his locker, he pulled out a stash of pharmaceutical morphine. He was kind enough to share.

You had deftly avoided promising Darla anything. Yet, the conversation had the air of a verbal contract. Inside your purse is a hermetically sealed hypodermic you purchased at Denver Drug

& Liquor, where the pharmacy clerks don't bother pretending that you're a diabetic. The supplies, you would argue, are for an emergency. Weddings are not all joy.

Shane, along with Jeremy and Ryan, takes drink orders for your table. There are ten of you—nearly a hundred pints of blood surging through thousands of miles of veins and arteries, the names and locations of which you memorized using an altered road map of Denver as a mnemonic device.

As you and the three men walk across the dance floor, the Rockies seem conveniently painted on the horizon, as if contracted and paid for. People at tables crane their necks at Darla and Quinn, who now make the expected rounds. Standing at the bar, Shane reluctantly lifts his camera to his eye.

"Let's get a picture," Jeremy says.

You stand between him and Ryan. Everyone smiles. "The three of you look like criminals," Shane says.

"Like famous criminals," you say.

You want to say that the human body contains endorphins that are two hundred times stronger than morphine. And yet, the cops never arrest anyone for endorphin possession.

You catch the bouquet only because: 1) you wear sensible shoes, Mary Janes, allowing you to jump higher than the other girls, and 2) Darla told you where she intended to throw the oversized daisies.

Shane catches the garter but then realizing the incestuous implication bobbles it into Jeremy's hands. The gesture makes everyone laugh, some *ooh* and *aah*, but now Shane looks at the garter in Jeremy's hands as if it's a sacred relic. His camera zooms in. As Jeremy slips the garter on your leg, he looks up at you, gives a sweet and embarrassed smile, and shrugs. You imagine what it might be like to kiss him.

A quick dance with Jeremy and Quinn cuts in. He's the groom and can cut in when he wants. When the song is over, you get a bottle of water from the bar and place it in your purse.

You share a cigarette with Quinn, and you tell him to appreciate the woman he has just married. He hugs you. "You know I will, Colleen," he says.

"You both look so happy," you say. Yet you can't help but notice the bags under his eyes. "Have you been sleeping?"

"I've been working hard on a campaign to save the forest down in Sandbench. The Forest Service has sold the old growth to loggers. I'm putting in long hours, and I'm afraid something more extreme than letter writing needs to occur."

In his suit, Jeremy hams a tap dance across the pavilion. He stops at a table where some of Darla's aunts, uncles, and cousins are seated. He pulls a flower from the vase in the center of the table and smiles. Dancing over to you and Quinn, he hands you the flower, and then takes it back. Snapping off the long stem, he pushes the orange daisy into your hair. "A posy for your red vines," he says.

"Be careful. You wouldn't want to cut your fingers on my rusty wires."

"I meant that as a compliment. Really," he says. "But you're trained to give me a tetanus shot, right?"

"I'll shoot you, all right," you say, making a gun with your hand and placing it against his temple. You have the sudden urge to take his pulse.

Jeremy slaps Quinn on the back. "I consider myself a wedding connoisseur and this is one hell of a wedding."

Across the pavilion, Darla stands alone, looking for Quinn. She sees him and smiles, beckons with a flourish of her now dirt-stained train. Quinn excuses himself and walks toward her with confident strides.

"She's a beautiful bride, but she doesn't hold a candle to you," Jeremy says.

For a moment, you consider telling him to get lost, but then you see something in his eyes, something that suggests he really means it. You feel color rising from your chest and up your neck.

Compliments can kill. People never think about how much it hurts to fall for someone.

Julius once told you that as death approaches—or has already encroached—people become sexually aroused. Two days ago, in the room of a dying man named George, you looked his wife in the eye and said that no one would disturb them. "I'll stand at the door," you said. "Knock when you're finished." George's funeral is today, and his name is written on a sticky note in Julius's locker.

"Beautiful sunset," Jeremy says. "It seems the universe might explode."

You ask him for a light, and with your thumb and index finger caress the orange petals in your hair. You feel like you might cry, though the causality is difficult to determine. Your friends' wedding? The death of a patient? The longing for a boy?

"What do you say we go for a boat ride?" Jeremy says. On the other side of the pavilion is a manmade pond with paddleboats.

"They don't rent them at night, do they?"

"Tonight they will," Jeremy says. "Hey, look. I'm sorry about our date. I wasn't very nice."

As the light changes, the rose garden is a kaleidoscope of shifting color and shade. You create a new rule, a series of rules. Let him look at your freckled face in the sunset. Let him wait and see how you change with every passing moment. Let every desire be a waiting. "Right," you say.

"I should have called, but I—"

"Didn't," you say.

"I didn't. I would like to. I still have your number, I mean."

Quiet. You turn toward the dance floor, where soft lights begin to flicker and brighten the pavilion. More kids are dancing than adults, although mothers and fathers hold the littlest ones in their arms, spinning round. So many tired and happy faces.

"Let's get another drink and go on a boat," he says.

"I need to use the toilet first," you say, which is true, but you also need a moment alone. The near cry and the sunset leave you with an empty feeling in your chest that can only be filled in one way. You take a deep breath and tell yourself that it wouldn't be right. After all, you nearly promised. You can wait until after the after-party—when you're home, in your dark apartment—to give in to your darker self.

In front of the bathroom mirror you push up your sleeve and with your thumb rub the needle bruises. Desiree stands behind you. When you look up, you jump and pull your sleeve back down.

"Sorry," she says. "I didn't mean to startle you."

You apply more concealer to a nonexistent zit. Desiree washes her hands. "My damn face," you say.

"What do you mean? That Irish skin," she says. She touches your cheek with the back of her hand, which smells like disinfectant soap. Even when a tear forms, you don't move.

"Thanks. I have faith in medicine," you say, and smile, holding up the small jar of cover-up.

"Jeremy's a good-looking young man," she says. "Go dance."

Twenty minutes later, you will walk across the dance floor with Jeremy, through the mothers and fathers dancing with their kids, the bride dancing with her father, and the groom dancing with his new mother-in-law. The receptors in your brain will have recalibrated and your body's interface will be in collusion with the world. You'll have the corrective in your blood. They'll play a love song by The Carpenters, and the bride will cry into her father's shoulder, as he sheds a few tears himself. Her mother will see the display and also begin to cry. Shane will capture the tears on film.

You'll smile when Jeremy spins you once on the dance floor. You'll take a silver spoon from one of the tables and slip it into your purse. You'll say, "Souvenir," and he'll wink and say, "Thief."

You'll both walk away from the party and toward the lake, where, before it seems possible, it is already dark.

Jeremy will give fifteen dollars to the teenager working at the boat dock and say that you might stay out awhile. They'll negotiate and Jeremy will give the kid another five dollars so that you can bring your drinks. You'll both agree on the green dragon over the pink flamingo.

When Jeremy pedals too fast, you'll explain the hydrodynamics of a paddleboat—how if you pedal too fast the paddle wheel has no resistance. With your left hand, you'll take his pulse at his neck, and with your right, you'll take his pulse at his elbow. He'll close his eyes for a moment and when he opens them he'll look at you as if you just saved his life. Slow and steady, you'll pedal out to what is called Bird Island.

The moon will be bright orange, almost a perfect circle. As the orb rises, it will shrink, but the two of you will soak in its Halloween glow. "The moon was full yesterday," you'll say. "After the rehearsal dinner, I watched it from my apartment when I was high."

"I'm not much of a smoker," he'll say, "but I saw it too."

"I wasn't smoking," you'll say.

You'll both pedal, turning the rudder occasionally to watch the moon shrink as it rises. Jeremy will pull out a flask and drink. He'll offer you some, but you'll decline. He'll lean in to kiss you, and you'll accept. With whiskey-wet lips, he'll say that he wished he had kissed you on the lame date. After he apologizes again, you'll tell him that it wasn't that big of a deal. He's not the first guy you've gone on a date with who made an ass out of himself. He'll hold your freckled fingers and just be nice.

"Can you keep a secret?" you'll say.

"Anything. As water splashes against the boat, you'll believe him.

"Do you mind if I shoot up?" you'll say. "Weddings make me—"

He'll nod, shrug his shoulders, lift his head to the moon, and take another pull of whiskey. "I won't tell a soul," he'll say.

You'll take out the lipstick case, the syringe, the elastic, the cotton ball, and the spoon. With the needle, you will suck up four cc's of water from the bottle, squeeze the water onto the spoon, and hand it to Jeremy. You will open the sealed plastic bag and then pinch the morphine onto the spoon. "Hold still," you'll say. As the spoon shakes in Jeremy's hand, you'll watch the flame and liquefying powder.

With the syringe, using the cotton as a filter, you'll suck the liquid from the spoon and tap it with your forefinger. Quickly, you'll push up your sleeve and wrap your bicep with the elastic. You'll take a deep breath and laugh when Jeremy holds his breath, too. He'll kiss you and you'll wish he hadn't, not right then. You'll find the cephalic vein opposite your elbow.

"You're a nurse," he'll say.

"In training," you'll say.

"You'll do fine," he'll say.

You'll push the needle in, hit, pull, hit, pull, and hit, the darkness hiding the fact that your blood swirling in the water/morphine mix looks like futuristic candy. You won't look at him, but you'll know that he's watching.

"Damn," he'll say. "I've actually never seen anyone..."

But you'll have stopped listening. You'll lean back against him, holding onto the green dragon with both hands and let the needle remain in your skin as it sways with the rocking of the boat. As you feel the rush come on, he'll kiss your rusty electric wires and it'll feel like something is falling through you, like he's fallen through you. "YMCA" will be playing far away, but the sound will clearly float across the water.

Jeremy will say, "Jesus, I love you," and even though you know he's drunk, you'll accept his prayers and give him your own in return.

You'll kiss him. His tongue will taste like ozone on velvet.

You'll say, "This is like dying."

He'll say, "But you'll be coming back. Won't you?"

"Promise me the last dance."
"I will," he'll say. "I will, I will, I will."
And you'll believe him.

LEGACY

ON MY FIFTEENTH BIRTHDAY, we celebrate with a small gathering of family and I hold the last unopened gift, what I know to be a rifle from my stepfather, the ridiculously named Anytime. He has been threatening to give me the rifle for nearly a year, starting right around the time he and my mother suggested that my sister and I take his last name, Vanderlay. Colleen and I chose to stay McMurphy.

Through the wrapping paper I can feel the barrel, stock, and trigger, but I heft around the still-wrapped rifle as if I have no clue what it is. My sister's best friend Darla, eyes glassy-red, twirls the candle in her mouth as you might a toothpick. Her hair is dripping wet, and I swoon in the intoxicating herbal fruit of her shampoo. Anytime is also distracted by Darla, so much so that he doesn't notice when I point the rifle at him.

"It's a gun!" shouts one of my little cousins. Everyone smiles, and Mom snaps a picture. Anytime makes a face that says, *Maybe it is, maybe it isn't.*

"Maybe it's an oar for a boat?" Colleen says, in her *I'm so terribly bored* voice. As soon as the party is over, Darla's driving Colleen and me to a kegger out at Gross Reservoir. My mother has never given her permission for me to go to a real party, but Colleen somehow convinced her. The party is Colleen's gift to me.

"Oh my, Shane, an oar!" Darla says, nearly climbing into Colleen's lap. "There's a gondola awaiting us. It's like we're in Venice, and you, as my personal gondolier, shall row me down the Boulder Creek!" She reclines across Colleen as if faint, one arm above her head, one around Colleen's neck, a light fuzz in her armpits. She has a way of making my head swim and my guts buzz. When she arrived at the house, Colleen whispered to me that Darla and her boyfriend, the hulking genius Quinn Mota, were on the outs, and Darla was thus stoned out of her mind on hydroponic weed grown by her parents, former rock stars turned organic farmers.

Her head hanging upside down off Colleen's lap, Darla says, "Have you ever been to Venice, Anytime?"

"Venice Beach? Like California?" Anytime says.

Anytime's German Shepard, Dick Lamm, named after our governor, licks Darla's upside-down face, and she jumps into a sitting position. "We're surrounded by beasts, dear! Somebody help."

I tear the paper from the rifle, trying to keep my face expressionless.

"I was right," my little cousin says. "I guessed it."

Anytime shaved his winter beard last week, and for the first time in six months you can see the fine print of his facial expression, and I take wry pleasure in the disappointment that resides there. "It's an over-under with both a .22 and a twenty-gauge barrel," Anytime says. Cameras flash. "My daddy gave me that rifle when I was about your age."

My mother shoots me a look that says she raised me with better manners. I wait a beat before I consent. "Thanks, Anytime." I turn it over in my hands and admire the swirled-wood grain of the stock. "It's really nice of you."

In his youth, Anytime had been a hippie but got drafted, and Vietnam left him with nervous tics. An autobody man, Anytime converted a section of the barn into his shop. Out by the driveway, there's one of those portable signs with an arrow on top that reads:

ANYTIME
PAINT & BODY WORK

A self-professed Renaissance man, Anytime also plays drums in a cover band called Grateful Airship. If you ask me, they tend to cover the worst of the Grateful Dead, Jefferson Airplane, and Jefferson Starship. If you ever meet Anytime, he'll tell you his life story in the first five minutes, including the fact that he played middle linebacker for the Boulder Panthers.

Anytime says that I'm too lazy for sports, but the truth is I prefer to do things that take patience and precision. I like to draw and I'm pretty good with my mother's camera. But the truth is, shooting is similar—it's seeing in a different way—peeling away all distractions and focusing. You've got to line things up so that they are true. Once, in a moment of genuine kindness, Anytime said I should take after him and be an autobody man. Cars don't really interest me much, and, besides, my mother and I agree that I should go to college and do something where I'll use my brains rather than my back.

There were rumors that the reason my dad left for Florida was that Anytime and my mother had a thing. Anytime has been married five times so rumors trail him like smoke does fire. He says that two of his marriages don't count. The first time he was eighteen, and it only lasted four weeks. One of the women he married twice. So before my mother, he only counts two wives. She's the third according to his math.

In a sloped field behind the house sits a target tacked to a hay bale, and beyond the field, the sun lowers itself behind Eldorado Mountain as if in burning shame. The mountain lifts from the high prairie floor, and from here you can see Devil's Thumb trying to hitch a ride, though one is never offered.

Anytime lectures me on the finer points of gun safety and routine cleaning. Having heard it all before, I nod my head absently. He tells me to hold the gun tight to my shoulder and to still my breathing. I hit near the bull's-eye. Anytime steps back, as if he's surprised that I hit the target at all. "I adjusted the sights for you," he says.

"I'm sure you did," I say. I pop off another one and it hits the center.

He sticks his hands in his armpits and smirks as if the gun itself does the aiming. His face turns sour when behind us Dick Lamm, chained to his coop adjacent to the barn, begins to bark and tug at his chain. "Guns send Dick Lamm hiding," Anytime says. "He must smell deer up there."

In the glow of the sunset, Dick Lamm continues to bark, and like a spark that sets a forest fire, up and down the valley dogs howl themselves crazy into the night that descends upon Eldorado Canyon.

We drive away in Darla's car, popping open cans of Coors before we're even past Anytime's sign at the end of the driveway. I am sitting in the middle of the backseat, where I have a forty-five degree view of Darla's profile, her tawny hair and faint spray of freckles.

"Do you feel more mature and/or manly now that you're armed?" Darla says.

"I'm not armed," I say, feeling as always like I don't quite get the joke.

"Too bad." She smiles and looks at me in the rearview. "You know way back my aunt used to date Anytime. She says that he packs a serious *pistol* if you catch my meaning." She shakes cigarettes out of a pack and all three of us light up. "But I guess he can't give away all of his arsenal."

"He is showing you fatherly attention," Colleen says. "Once you master the art of marksmanship, I think he'll ask you to join the band."

"As a break dancer!" Darla takes her hands from the wheel and speaks into her fist. "Grateful Starship featuring Shane McBeats."

"To hell with that," I say. "I don't want to be in his jackoff band. If he wanted a dancer, he'd ask you. He can't keep his eyes off you."

"I am a better dancer than you, and Anytime is sort of cute without that beard," Darla says.

"Oh vomit," Colleen says. Her good humor is gone, and she stares out the window. We share the ability to disappear the outside world and vanish into the smoke of the self. I press my foot into the back of Darla's seat, kicking it slowly and repeatedly. "Okay! Okay! No more talk about Anytime's cuteness." I give another kick. "Or his pistol," she says, laughing.

At Gross Reservoir, there is not much light, save for the stars and the fire started with beer boxes and fueled with driftwood, though you can still see the silhouetted mountains that hang like a black curtain. People stand around the fire swallowing beer and mouthing words that slip over the lake.

Darla stands on a cliff edge that rises about ten feet above the water, and below her is an inky pool of reflected fire. There is no way to tell the deep water from where a rock might be lurking below the surface. A few people stand with her, coaxing and convincing. My sister says, "Don't be stupid."

The commotion gets everyone looking at Darla. I've been watching her all night. I've been watching her for years, though it has always seemed that she is far older and more experienced than I am. When she was just a kid and her parents were touring they crisscrossed the country in a yellow van, and maybe it was on the road that she developed her courage and her brashness.

Darla turns toward the crowd and clasps her hands into a single fist, raised high above her head. People call out in succession. "Jump!" "Naked!" "Geronimo!"

Darla studies the water, her hands at her sides. The fire dances in shadow tattoos on her flesh. She pushes off the rock, diving at a steep angle, and cuts the water's surface. There is a burst of laughter and shouting, and then everything is quiet. The water sloshes against the cliffs. When Darla doesn't surface, there is a sudden quiet, a few whispers. I wonder what it's like to be the water all wrapped around Darla, her gliding right through you.

I'm not worried like the others because I know she doesn't have things happen to her—Darla happens to others.

Darla explodes from the surface and screams like a banshee. The laughter and the hollering start again. There is a great move to the cliff face, and one after another they jump feet first into the water.

Back on shore, Darla dries her face on Colleen's shirt. "Get off me." Colleen's eyes are wet, and she sucks at her lips. "There's not a single reason why that was a good idea." Colleen shrinks away from Darla, turns, and disappears into the darkness.

Darla shrugs. Standing next to the fire, she shakes her head back and forth, like a wet dog, throwing orange sparks of water on everyone within ten feet. I take off my flannel shirt and give it to her.

"Come here," she says. "Keep a look-out while I take a squirt." We walk along the shore a little ways until we come across a Volkswagen-sized boulder. I keep my back to the rock and listen to her rush of water spraying the ground. "That's better," she says, coming out from behind the rock and snapping the button on her shorts. "Sit down and have a smoke with me, birthday boy."

We sit on a ledge that looks down on the revelers on the shore and in the water. It's peaceful up here away from the talking faces, their voices melting into one another as if heated by the fire. The snap of a burning log splits the drone of voices and simultaneously Darla scoots so close to me that through my jeans I can feel the gooseflesh on her leg. We sit like this a minute, then she says, "Let's take a drive, birthday boy."

We drive far enough to share a cigarette and find a dirt road, where she pulls over onto a wide shoulder. Darla kisses me hard, her lips night-swimming cold, and the inside of her mouth is the softest kind of warm I can imagine. We've kissed before during a game or two of Truth or Dare, but this hardly compares. "Happy birthday, cutie. It's your party," she says. "You can do what you want to." She pulls my shirt over my head and then removes her own. I consider Quinn Mota for a moment, and I imagine his fist connecting with my face. But then her breast is in my hand, in my mouth, and soon I am doing things that I had only ever imagined.

We light a cigarette and I think about returning to the party. I imagine Quinn Mota or one of his buddies pushing an accusatory finger into my chest. I imagine my inability to defend myself, the inevitable humiliation. I dare to kiss Darla one more time. Trying not to sound like a coward, I say, "I've got curfew."

Darla's rust bucket hugs the winding roads, and with the windows up anything seems possible. We hit a pothole and the result is that the car sounds sub-sonic, drowning out all other sounds. Vibrations come up through the seat and the floorboards. We pull over and I shine a flashlight on the muffler that has decoupled from the catalytic convertor. It doesn't stop us from driving home and pulling into the driveway with the lowest and loudest rumbling sound imaginable.

We sit on the patio behind the kitchen, polishing off the beers that remain in the cooler. I see our reflection in the sliding-glass door, and we look like jolly good fools—beer, birthday cake, and rifle propped up in an Adirondack chair.

"I had a nice time tonight," I say. A pack of wild dogs or coyotes yelps across the ridge behind the house.

"*Nice?*" she says.

Dick Lamm stirs in his coop. His chain rattles and he whines submissively.

"Great. I meant great, awesome, the best. Like I would like to do it again."

"Shane?" Darla narrows her eyes and studies my face for a moment, seemingly trying to communicate something that I am probably too stupid and too lovesick to understand. "Dogs or coyotes?" she says.

"Coyotes, I hope."

"There's a real wild dog problem these days, as if the freedom is too enticing for your everyday domestic dog."

"I would be willing to give it a shot," I say, hoping she understands *it* to mean *us.*

"You're too sweet to be a wild dog."

Quinn Mota's Nova pulls into the driveway. He walks directly up to Darla and, ignoring me, says, "Let's go."

"We're having some beer," Darla says, sounding drunker than she did a moment before. Quinn wears thick glasses and an olive field-patrol cap. He yanks Darla to her feet. "Fuck you!" she says.

"You're going to make a scene?" Quinn says flatly.

I struggle to lift myself out of the Adirondack chair. "What's your problem?" I say. With one hand still holding Darla's wrist, Quinn shoves me with his free hand, sending me toppling over the chair, birthday cake and rifle spilling from the adjoining table and chair.

The kitchen light switches on, and I look to see Anytime in his skivvies. He's as a tall as Quinn, though he's bulkier at his age. He slides the door open and walks out, not the least bit self-conscious. "Problem?" he says.

"No problem here, sir," Quinn says.

I'm on my feet again and Anytime gives me a look-over, glances at the rifle and the birthday cake. "It's probably time to end this little party. Quinn, get your car out of my driveway. Darla, you woke the house with that muffler. Shane, clean up this mess and then get your ass in bed."

Without a word, Darla and Quinn walk away and start their cars. Anytime and I watch them leave and wince at the sound of Darla's exhaust. Anytime walks to the sliding glass doors and before he's completely inside he says, "Your mother worked a long time on that cake."

In the morning, Anytime and I walk together through the warmth of the summer woods, not saying much, but when we do it's in whispers. The smell of cedar is stronger than our voices. Anytime says we wouldn't normally walk in a pair. It's my first time out, though, and he wants to make sure I'm doing things right. You have to step quietly and keep your eyes and ears open. I know he doesn't much care for small game—he would rather be out hunting deer or bear. I'm not old enough to get a big-game license, so he's stuck with me, maybe getting a shot off at a rabbit, or even worse, a squirrel. I ask Anytime if when he's hunting he's reminded of Vietnam. He looks at me as if I'm crazy. Sometimes I think he might have been one of those nutty bastards, like in the movies, who got so wound up that he started setting villages on fire.

Anytime touches his hand to the barrel of my gun, and we stop walking. "Hear that?" he says in a voice so soft it's like the green moss on the rocks. Branches and dead leaves scrape and shift from a scraggly blackberry bush about fifty feet away. I raise my gun and sight it on the bush. Everything is quiet, and I taste last night's beer in my mouth. I see a long, gray ear appear out of the left side of the blackberry bush. The rabbit hops out of hiding, and before I can get a sight on him, he's off. I lead him, just like Anytime taught me, still my breath, and squeeze the trigger. The gray body flips over on its side.

"Sonofabitch! Told you. That rifle's a damn legacy."

I remember to breathe again when Anytime slaps me on the back. The rabbit is fat, and there is a red hole at the base of the skull. "Do the honors," Anytime says, pulling a knife from a sheath on his belt. "Just cut up from the asshole," he says. I squat in front of the rabbit and make the gut. A handful of naked bunnies fall out on the dead leaves. "Ah, shit," Anytime says. Like tired puppets, bodies alive though barely moving.

"Can we?" I say, looking up at Anytime. "I could raise them," I say.

"Absolutely not. We're not running a petting zoo."

I feel like a child for even asking the question. I hand the knife to Anytime, and he wipes it on his boot bottom. Lightly, with the pad of my skinny index finger, I touch one of the hairless bunnies, hoping that the gesture will be revelatory, that it will speak to these small creatures. But it doesn't feel like much at all.

"They're too small to live, Shane." Anytime puts his hand on my shoulder.

I flip over a rock about the size of the dead mother and into the hole I place the dying litter. I fit the rock back over the soft pile, wincing and wishing I had covered them with dirt. Still, the rock should save them from Dick Lamm or other animals.

We walk home through a field of timothy, our legs wet with dew, the dead rabbit hanging upside from my hand. Anytime pauses and turns to me. He says, "You're old enough to make your own decisions. And I sure as hell am not here to tell you about the birds and the bees." He looks down toward the house and glances at the rabbit in my hand. He's stalling. "I know she's your sister's friend, but I would encourage you to stay away from that girl."

"What?" I say, uncertain how Anytime would know about what happened.

"Boy, I could smell it on you when I walked outside last night!"

"Smell what?"

"Okay. Play dumb all you want, but when Colleen got home last night, she was not very happy. She said you and Darla drove off together."

"So?"

"The women in Darla's family make a hobby out of throwing men under the bus. I should know because I once had what I thought was a serious thing with her aunt."

"We just went for a drive."

"She and her boyfriend break up, she hops in the backseat with her best friend's brother, and then the boyfriend shows up immediately afterward? It doesn't take rocket math to figure this one out, and if you can't see that, your vision's clouded by hormone mist."

"Here's your rabbit," I say. I hand it to him amidst his protests. I walk through the field alone, the sun burning bright on my anger.

The days go by, and when no one is around, I call Darla, who never seems to be home. I ignore Colleen until I can take it no more, and when my mother and Anytime are at church, I knock on her door. I hear The Smiths "How Soon is Now?" playing on her boom box. I stand with my ear against the door, listening to the hypnotizing sadness of the vibrato guitar and Morrissey crooning about being the heir to nothing.

I knock and she says, "Don't creep at my door," as if she has seen me standing there. I open the door but remain in the doorway. Sitting on her bed, her hair an explosion of cinnamon curls, she wears an oversized baseball jersey and she is painting her toenails black. An ashtray sits on the windowsill above the bed and smoke from a joint spirals upward and out the screen.

"If Mom caught you smoking dope in your room while they were at church, she would kill you."

"How exactly is she going to catch me if she's in church?"

"Maybe the same way that Anytime found out that—"

"That you fucked my best friend?"

"What difference does it make to you?"

"I'm the one who convinced Mom to let you go." She points at me with the nail polish brush. "They're *my* friends anyway."

"Do you think she's a slut?"

"You moron. I thought I taught you better, but you're just like all the rest. Every women is either slut, tease, or prude. Get out!" She winds up and throws a lighter that I deflect using the door as a shield.

—

From outside Anytime's shop, I hear a wild giggle that I know to be Darla's. Even though he's a body man, Anytime has agreed to fix Darla's muffler. Along with Darla's laugh is Anytime's low *haw-haw*. It's been a week since the party, and she hasn't said a word about what happened that night. I want to tell her that I love her, but I know better.

I cannot resist the urge to stand outside the door and continue to listen. Dick Lamm walks up beside me, looks at me accusingly. I am the creep that my sister insists that I am. Anytime grunts every once in a while, like he does when he's turning wrenches. I get my head to where I can see. The car is elevated on ramps. Darla's leaning into the trunk, apparently looking for something.

With a tailpipe in his hands, Anytime comes up behind her. He says, "If you were looking for something on the side, you should have asked a real man." He slips the pipe between her legs.

Darla jumps up in the air, and says, "Watch it, goddammit." She gives Anytime an angry look that soon transforms into a smirk. Anytime shrugs his big shoulders.

My knees feel soft and my gut burns. For some reason I'm almost crying but it's because I'm remembering the first time I ever went to Florida and rode a roller coaster at Circus World— Dad was still with us, and my grandmother came along on the trip. I was only eight. We ate salami sandwiches at the rest stops. At night, my mother would go to bed early so she could drive the first shift. Colleen and I watched cable TV, which was a treat since we only get three channels on the mountaintop. Dad and my grandmother would drink beer, smoke cigarettes, and play cards long after everyone was asleep. Those nights with all five of us packed into a single room, I slept like I've never slept before or since.

Dogs yelp into the silence. Darla and Anytime turn to see me standing at the door. The yelping continues, off behind the barn in the narrow field. The sounds are like crazy people laughing, and then I see the pack of six brown and black dogs, surrounding a deer. Dick Lamm takes off toward the pack and the deer.

"Dick Lamm!" Anytime screams. "Goddamnit! Git back here!" Dick Lamm ignores his master, and Anytime runs after him. "Shane! Get the gun and come on!"

Darla stares at me, and she looks scared. I run into the house, grab the rifle, and throw some shells into my pocket. The deer, the dogs, and Anytime have made it a good way down the field. I catch up to them as the deer runs up a knoll. The dogs, including Dick Lamm, are just a few yards behind. Anytime, doing a poor job of keeping up, runs up the knoll. I jog behind and stop at the bottom of the green hill. The deer continues up an opening that follows the power lines. On either side are the woods. Only the dogs will be able to keep up once the deer decides to head into the trees.

"Shoot the fucking gun!" Anytime jumps up and down, waving his arms. He doesn't want to see his dog run away and get shot. "Shoot! Shoot!"

I lift the gun to my shoulder. It is a straight line from me to Anytime to the dogs to the deer. I sight the gun and Anytime's bigness is right there. He looks at me funny, and his hands drop to his sides. He tilts his head like Dick Lamm does when he's in trouble. I wonder if Anytime feels like he is in Vietnam now. I keep the sight on Anytime for a second longer, but I'm not sure why. I lower the gun and wonder if I'll be like him when I get older. Not that I'd be a mechanic, but that I'll just be plain mean. The deer is still running full-tilt up the hill, and I watch it until I can only see its mountain ghost of a white tail disappear into the forest. I look back at Darla and she is standing, her hands covering her nose and mouth, as if she were praying. I hold the gun with both hands. It has a weight I don't seem to remember.

MERCY COMES CALLING

MELISSA WAS A WAITRESS BY PROFESSION and, it seemed to her, by cosmic design. She waited tables. She waited on her twin sons, London and Paris. She was waiting on divorce papers. And now she was reluctantly waiting for her grandmother to die.

From the time that Melissa first possessed the curiosity to eavesdrop on her grandmother's telephone conversations, she believed the woman justifiably insane by reason of neighbors, deceased husband, children, and a flock of churches that she had joined and then foresworn. "One trespass was all it took to fall the paradise of Eden," Chloris Burns would say, "and nowadays people don't even recognize their own shame. It's no wonder I'm brainsick." Melissa imagined the sickness as something like Silly Putty within her grandmother's brain, stretched and distorted by the insults and injuries the world thrust upon her. Melissa assumed that she carried the trait, and for this reason, she not only humored her grandmother, but offered her genuine sympathy. She knew all her grandmother's stories, which like most detailed the storyteller's suffering and self-sacrifice. Even if she was bragging on Melissa (as she often did) Chloris might begin: "I had three daughters—each a different kind of disappointment—but my granddaughter here…"

Chloris's eldest had married a Texas real estate agent and raised three daughters in a pretentiously large house that Chloris only knew from pictures. Chloris's middle child was on her fourth marriage. The youngest, Melissa's mother, had served twelve of a twenty-two-year sentence down in Cummins after pleading not guilty, though Chloris supposed she was. Chloris had droned on endlessly about how she had been marked with a palpable shame by her daughter's crimes. It wasn't until she battled the state of Arkansas for custody of Melissa and won that she knew she had been redeemed. Overnight Chloris's shame hardened into a defiant and prideful glint in her eyes that dared anyone to question the child's disposition. But even then, at thirteen-years-old, Melissa had a deserved reputation as a jailbird's chick: skipping rope one day and the next sitting in some no-account's pickup and blowing cigarette smoke out the window. Chloris would confront Melissa with rumors of her misdeeds, and, through an elaborate process of lies, gullibility, and selective belief, they invariably came to the conclusion that Melissa was relatively blameless but did frequently find herself adrift in the currents of boredom and bad influence.

A week before, a Little Rock doctor had pronounced Chloris's cancer terminal, giving her only weeks to live, and now Melissa was driving them home. They rode in silence until out of nowhere Chloris said, "Lamar Asa Hodges is, by birth and character, a carpetbagger and a charlatan."

It was true, Melissa thought. The fact was she did enjoy a good wrestle with Lamar in the back of the Cordoba, though she didn't care to talk about it with her grandmother. "I wish you would reconsider the hospice care," Melissa said.

"You should break it off with that man so that I can die in peace."

"Barbara's mother had real good luck with hospice."

"No one has *good luck* with hospice! They all die. Quackery, I say. Turn here. I want you to drive me to Delashmits'. I'm going to make my own arrangements. I won't have you and Florine pricing caskets while Rose Dawn and her clan root through my dresser drawers and my tackle boxes."

"Rose Dawn don't give a whit for what's in your tackle boxes."

"It's yours is what I'm trying to say," Chloris said. Now they both fought back tears and Chloris said, "I imagine death is like a doorway that I've got no choice but to step through." Melissa drove between the wrought-iron gates of the Delashmit Funeral Home, a wave of vertigo overtaking her as she pictured Chloris on one side of death's door and herself on the other.

Melissa Delashmit stood by, hiding her smile behind a hand, as Chloris harangued Maynard, her soon-to-be ex-husband. Before Melissa had kicked him to the curb, Maynard had adamantly refused to be a part of the family business, but something had happened to him after Melissa asked him to leave. Most folks believed it was for the better, though Chloris didn't see it that way.

"Maynard, after the way you humiliated my granddaughter, you and your father owe me a reasonably priced funeral." Maynard pulled at his collar like he was a fish that managed to catch itself. Jaundice pooled in Chloris's eyes, and she clamped her yellow tongue between her lips. "I'll handle the posies, the music, and the programs, but I'll be damned to pay those prices for an ash urn or a box rental. I've got my own photographer, too. Jimmy's boy is coming down from Colorado. I've talked to him myself, and he's a gentleman. Shane McMurphy's his name. He's Irish, not a drop of Eastern European blood. And he's American Indian, too, which is kind of erotic if you think about it."

"I think you mean exotic, Granma."

"Never you mind. Melissa thinks I'm morbid to hire a funeral photographer, but these days a funeral's more permanent than a wedding, and surely no Christian would marry without a photographer. To tell the truth, I think they'd make a fine pair. Melissa, as you know, Maynard, was well on her way to becoming a professional photographer until you came along."

Melissa had been a photography major at the University of Arkansas when she married Maynard, and after she discovered herself pregnant she had dropped out upon his request. She had imagined a photography studio in town—portraits and weddings more than funerals. But Jimmy bragged that his son was no run-of-the-mill photographer. His son's pictures had been in glossy magazines and art shows, leaving Melissa to wonder why such a hotshot would take funeral work. Chloris said that it was because he had a generous spirit, like her own. It wasn't like Chloris to go to so much trouble, which led Melissa to believe that she was indeed playing matchmaker.

The old woman explained to Maynard that after the visitation, she would be cremated, despite (or, perhaps, owing to) the Catholic birds from Monday Night Bingo and their infernal debates about whether or not cremation interferes with God resurrecting the body. "I've never quite picked apart the knots of God's rules and regulations, but I'm certain enough of my own character that God, decent and competent as He is, will not refuse me a seat in heaven based on whether I'm cremated, embalmed, or mummified for that matter." And with that, the dying woman led Melissa by the arm out of the funeral parlor and back to the car.

They lived in a copse of mobile homes facing Lake Conway, where sixty years back Arkansas Game and Fish had declared eminent domain and flooded almost seven thousand acres of the Palarm Bottoms, a stretch of swamp and hardwoods. A hundred of those acres, Chloris reasoned, had been swiped from the Burns family. The Lake Conway Project had been spearheaded by Martin Hodges, the grandfather of Lamar, the carpetbagger and charlatan and owner of the Cordoba that Melissa so enjoyed getting naked inside.

These days, bald cypress rose from the shallow lake. The old woman's home was an assemblage of additions that hid a twelve-by-sixty-eight trailer parked on cinderblocks in '67, and flanking hers was Florine and Jimmy's on one side and on the other Melissa's peach-colored singlewide.

Chloris still considered the underwater ninety-five acres rightfully hers—Melissa stood to inherit it all. Before her illness,

Chloris would, at least once daily, check her yo-yos rigged with chicken livers, and now for the last time, Chloris sat in her flat-bottom, navigating for Melissa, who steered from one rigged bald cypress to the next. Chloris pulled in two catfish and a turtle, and Melissa took pictures. With Chloris offering unnecessary instructions, Melissa nailed the first catfish to a cypress and the second to a tar-covered piling. "I know you think I'm crazy," Chloris said, "but a no-trespassing sign's got nothing on the power of a crucified catfish."

When they reached the shore, Chloris was exhausted and unable to lift herself from the boat. "I worry if I'll have strength to walk through that door when it's presented."

"You're tired is all." Melissa suggested fetching Jimmy and Florine to help, but Chloris stopped her. "We've always done for each other," Chloris said. "You've got to tap your vigor, dear. You'll need it when the time comes."

"I wish you wouldn't talk that way," Melissa said. For years her grandmother had insisted that she would not be a vegetable at the hands of quackery, and that, if Melissa cared, she would show her mercy.

"They was about to put you in a foster home, but I opened my arms."

"I might have lived with Florine."

"There's a reason, Melissa, why the Lord salted her womb. You're more like me than any of my girls. My good looks and sense of mercy skipped a generation." Melissa stood in the water and lifted Chloris to the shore. She prayed for Chloris to go in her sleep.

Melissa was finishing up a double shift at Catty's Fish House, feeling as if she had been soaked in milk and dipped in cornmeal herself, like the three-piece catfish special "The Snag." Her life in two words, she thought, especially since Chloris's condition had quickly worsened. She was in indescribable pain, though she hadn't touched drugs in her life—not even an aspirin—and she refused to start. On several occasions, Melissa had walked into Chloris's room to hear her muttering a prayer that went *Mercy, mercy, mercy.* She would quiet when Melissa pressed a cold washcloth to her head, but then Melissa found herself wishing that Chloris would just go—walk through the goddamn door, or whatever the hell death was. When Chloris would finally sleep, peacefully it seemed, Melissa thought her own cynical lapse a kind of betrayal to the woman she loved as much as anyone.

Melissa wiped down the tabletops checkered with the laminated advertisements for realtors and AC salesmen and one of a smiling idiot father-and-son team of undertakers. She tossed her washrag into a bleach bucket and said, "Anyone else think Maynard's new moustache looks like a Halloween disguise?" The other waitresses laughed and one said, "More like a *pornstache.*" Six months before, Maynard had filed a police report claiming that his credit card had been stolen and that $3,600 had been charged in the Ukraine. His name had appeared in the police beat section of the newspaper, and the girls at Catty's had had a field day teasing Melissa about Maynard's Ukrainian bride. When he was about to leave with the bags she had hurriedly packed for him, she couldn't resist one final jab: "Maynard, could you even find the Ukraine on a map?" He didn't say a word, but he looked at her as if she had asked if he knew where we go after we die. Though she had known that the Ukraine was in Europe, she had to Google it herself to pinpoint the exact location. She knew where Maynard was most nights—she could see the lights of the log home he rented across the lake. It wasn't so much that he wanted to keep track of her as it was that he couldn't do without the fishing.

Melissa looked up from marrying the Louisiana hot sauce bottles to find Catty's owner, Barbara, shaking her head. "Young woman, I pray that God will call you and yours and offer rebirth."

"Once is enough, thank you," Melissa said. Barbara, a Primitive Baptist, prayed that all of her waitresses—Christian, heathen, and strumpet alike—were cast among the elect, but Melissa, in particular, tested Barbara's optimistic sense of predeterminism. After the other girls left for home, Barbara said, "I've been praying for your grandmother. I'm sorry she's not improving."

"Maybe you've got the wrong number," Melissa said, "or maybe He's just not listening."

Barbara leaned her full weight against the cash counter. She wore thick glasses and her back had a pronounced hump. "Burns women have never known humility. Your grandmother used to show you off, saying that you was *spun from gold*, though no Burns ever had two nickels to rub together."

"We get by just fine," Melissa said, "just because we don't spend our lives—"

"You're a tough lot, that's for sure, and though you smile and sweet-talk customers all day long, I see the strain around your lips and the fear in your eyes."

Her timecard shaking in her hand, Melissa snorted a laugh and walked through the door before hitting the overhead lights and leaving Barbara in the dark with the Mexican dishwashers she never much trusted.

At home, she checked on the twins, who were sleeping at Jimmy and Florine's. She walked across the yard to her grandmother's where, for the last two weeks, Florine, Jimmy, or Melissa herself had been on constant deathwatch. "I don't think she'll last much longer," Florine said. "Her breath ain't much more than a whisper."

Melissa was asleep on the couch when Chloris called out, her voice strong. "Melissa, it's time." In the yellow lamplight, Melissa was entranced by Chloris's pleading eyes. Chloris's scabbed lips didn't move, but Melissa had the strange sensation that she could hear her voice: *It's nothing but a doorway, but I hadn't suspected how painful it would be to cross the threshold.* With something that Melissa imagined was telepathy, Chloris asked her for a shove. Melissa picked up a pillow from the rocker and only then did death descend on Chloris Burns, death like a downy cloud dropping from the ceiling. Melissa kept her eyes closed and a shudder rose from Chloris's body, a rhythmic flapping, like a bird taking flight. Eyes still closed, Melissa saw a burst of eyelid red, the door that Chloris had conjured, though she didn't see Chloris herself. When Melissa opened her eyes, she dropped to the floor and felt like she was falling from a never-ending height.

After a day of tears with Florine, Melissa asked her aunt to watch the boys and she left to meet Lamar. She felt a sexual hunger that she couldn't quite explain. Perhaps her body instinctively knew that sex might quell the hurt. Under the last full moon of the spring, she drove along Lake Conway, the dead cypress branches looking like arms that reached toward a light at the end of some forsaken tunnel. Burning garbage scorched the night. She passed the dock with the sign that read *ONE NATION UNDER GOD!*, gravel popping beneath her tires like angry doubt.

A week after she had kicked Maynard out, Lamar had sat in a booth at Catty's and ordered "The Snag." He had asked Melissa if she knew about what they called the Monty Hall Problem, but she only remembered that Chloris loved *Let's Make a Deal*. A classic Hodges grin on his face, he flashed three of his business cards, each printed with *Lamar Asa Hodges: Buck of the Odds*. Melissa knew that Lamar was a bookie, though she didn't care to know the scope or scale of his illegal endeavors. On the blank side of one business card, he printed an *M* and, in shell-game fashion, moved the cards—*Buck of the Odds* side up—about the table. He promised her a prize, anything she liked, so she pointed. He flipped over a different card, blank, no *M*, and slid it into his pocket. This left the card she chose and another sitting on the table. "You now get a chance to change your choice. The rules of chance say that you should. It's a veridical paradox. I've been studying this here Monty Hall Problem in my games and gambling class. I won't be stuck forever working at my uncle's sign shop. Do you want to change your choice or not?" She had no idea what he was talking about. "Lamar, you don't even know what I want for a prize." He winked and she changed her choice. He flipped the card to reveal the *M*. "So what you want, Melissa Burns?"

"My name's been Delashmit for five years," she said. She was hesitant to answer such a question. Melissa looked up from the table and saw Barbara perched at the cash register, flashing Melissa accusatory looks. She said, "I need to finish my side work, Lamar." She liked him, maybe because he was wild, maybe because he wasn't Maynard. When she didn't move, he smiled as if he could read her mind. "Granma says that every Hodges is born with a smug look on his face."

"Most people are satisfied playing the hand that's dealt them, but we Hodges' have a natural inclination for stirring the pot and picking the winners." He flipped a twenty on the table, and when she reached for it, he grabbed her hand. "Melissa, you won, so you got to tell me what you want." Most of what she wanted were *didn't wants*—she *didn't want* to have a mother mean enough to commit manslaughter, *didn't want* Chloris dying, *didn't want* a soon-to-be ex-husband who sent money to a Ukrainian Internet hustler. She *didn't want* to disappoint Lamar, not when she had nothing else and not when he might provide her the perfect revenge on Maynard. "How about a ride in that fancy car of yours?" she said. Barbara, who still stood staring from her cash register, audibly clucked.

That night, as soon as Melissa had walked in her front door, she had picked up the ringing phone to hear Chloris's voice. "For near all of my life, Hodges' have been trying to sink me, and now Lamar—the biggest fool of them all—is after my little girl's heart." Melissa had casually denied that she had a heart to steal but did not deny Lamar. "Granma, Martin Hodges has been dead for over twenty years." Later, she never admitted to how much she saw Lamar—after-work rolls in his car, occasional Saturday nights spent drinking beer at the VFW—nor how little Lamar wanted to do with the boys, who he believed looked like two miniature versions of Maynard.

When Melissa drove up on Lamar and his car, she hit the brakes. Lamar stood in a cloud of dust, the freshly waxed car shining behind him. "You should pay me the attention you pay that car"

"It's not just a car, Melissa. It's a *Cordoba*." Lamar held her shoulders, hands stinking of paint and gasoline fumes. "I'm sorry about your gran-gran," he said. The cicadas and frogs sang a fevered pitch. Twenty feet from where they stood, Lamar had stacked a small pyramid of cans—paint and paint thinner, and with uncanny accuracy flipped his cigarette, sparking the thinner. "A memorial blaze," he said.

"Lamar, now you've got me thinking about how she's going to be cremated."

"I didn't know that," he said.

"Well, she is, but I didn't come out here to talk about it." She placed her hand against his zipper. Lamar smiled in that way that said he had done too many bad things to list.

"Darlin', every fire I set is to make Melissa Burns hot."

"My name hasn't been Burns since my wedding day."

"And I was a groomsman. Goes to show that we're all at the mercy of chance."

"Mercy?"

"Well, yeah? You know, like we're powerless against it."

"She kept praying *mercy*—"

"I thought you didn't want to talk about her."

"She asked me, Lamar…"

"Melissa, I'm happy to talk if you need to talk, but you're sending mixed messages to the boner I'm developing."

In the backseat of the Cordoba, desire overtaking her fatigue and her guilt, she clenched her body against Lamar's. She pushed him back and reached to the floor to grab a pen from her apron. When he saw the pen, Lamar imitated Ricardo Montalbán's accent from the 1975 Cordoba ads he was always watching on YouTube: "Careful of the soft Corinthian leather." Melissa put the pen to his bare chest and in block letters she wrote *SHAME*. A paint can blew and they groaned.

He'd leave her writing on his chest for weeks. He always did. He was dim, she thought, but he was sentimental, too.

Melissa stood at the visitation shaking hands, receiving embraces, shedding tears. She sat when dizzy, and when the vertigo passed, she stood on platform shoes. She thought *visitation* the wrong word for this gathering. You had a visitation from a ghost or a space alien. This was just a *visiting*. It was neighbors and members of the many churches Chloris had joined and fled. It was Rose Dawn's clan from Texas; Barbara and the waitresses from Catty's; Florine and Jimmy's friends; Maynard's extended family. She longed to be with the twins, snuggling and watching a feature-length cartoon and eating popcorn. Instead, she collected looks of sympathy and pity, said, *Thank you for coming, Thank you for coming, Thank you for coming*. She kept her crying in check by tracking the motion of the funeral photographer, who seemed to move about the room with a quiet grace. His face was all sharp angles, eyes the color of pecan meat, dark hair hanging limp over his ears. He reminded Melissa of men from Depression-era photos, men that looked like chronic strangers.

After was coffee and cake and lite beer with the family at Florine and Jimmy's, and when the dull conversations pained her too much, Melissa walked outside into a twilight that was pink and gray, a light she thought perfect for disappearing. Barefoot in the dew-damp grass, Melissa leaned against the outdoor stone-

and-mortar fireplace, a finger of smoke rising from the chimney. The funeral photographer walked out onto the porch and looked at Melissa. She wondered if she looked to him like a woman whose house had been reduced to ashes, the fireplace the only thing left standing.

Shane McMurphy lifted his camera and said, "Do you mind? The light, this time of day, the water. It's hard to resist." He walked from the porch and slowly turned in a circle, pausing several times as if framing images—the greening cypress in the lake, two flat-bottomed boats and a canoe bobbing on the shoreline, ivy strangling garden gnomes—but his gaze was drawn back to Melissa, her hair, eyes, and skin slight variations of golden bronze, toenails painted turquoise.

She pointed down the gravel road at a half-torched and rotted trailer, its exposed living room like a black mouth, yellow insulation hanging from the underside. The lawn littered with a miniature plastic slide, a rusted tricycle, and a camouflage-painted riding mower. "It was three o'clock in the morning, months ago," she said, "when fire trucks came howling and those two hollering on whose fault it was." She made a sound of derisive laughter. "Welcome to the neighborhood."

"I've photographed New Orleans after Katrina, and a town in eastern Colorado reduced to matchsticks by tornadic winds."

"All that between funerals?" she said. He looked insulted, which she had intended, though she guessed she didn't have anything against him—at least he showed sense enough to get away from coffee-slurping mourners. "I got a relation in Colorado. Mack Taitt. He used to sort of be a famous rock musician, and now he's a drunk farmer."

"You're related to Mack Taitt?"

"He doesn't have anything to do with our side of the family. Too good for us."

"Funeral photography may seem strange now, but I think that later you'll appreciate the photographs. There is something about capturing the unraveling of life." He pulled a flask from his hip pocket and they shared sips of vodka, and she resisted telling him that he was full of shit. "I mostly did this as a favor to my father. He was a big fan of your grandmother's. I was too, really. We had several conversations about her desire for funeral photographs, but the conversations usually came back to you."

"Don't believe a word of what she said. She was a crazy old crow." A bit drunk, Melissa led Shane along the banks of the lake to what London and Paris called their island. The moon sat low and cypress cast shadows on the lake. Dogs barked, a country bass line thumped amphibian-like, and insects buzzed an orgy of desire, exciting and sad, a muddle of love and lust. "I was studying to be a photographer," she said. He asked what stopped her and she said, "A husband that got me pregnant."

"London and Paris. How can you even tell them apart?" He winced, even before she gave him a look that suggested the countless times she had heard the question.

"I named them for the princess honeymoon I always wanted, where me and my prince would fly to London and then take the Chunnel to Paris. I've never flown before." She blushed and felt a nervous wave, the anxiety of pending anxiety, and lit a cigarette. "I get vertigo something awful, so we went to Lake Dardanelle, which, big deal, is an hour from here. Maynard's big surprise was a driving tour of Europe in Arkansas. Lunch in London. Ice cream in Dublin. We stayed in Paris at the Paris Inn. All in Arkansas, and for Maynard it's about as romantic as it gets." She told him how she had wanted the real Europe, but they didn't have the money, and even if they had, Maynard said he wouldn't fly with her, not with her fear of heights. "Maynard never understood vertigo's power over me. How can you explain to someone? *No, it doesn't feel like I'm falling. I* am *falling.*"

"I once photographed a wedding, but I was in love with the bride. It was Mack Taitt's daughter, Darla."

"Get out! You were in love with my cousin?"

The entire time, I felt lightheaded, like I'd fall at any moment. My first funeral gig in a way. She got the marriage annulled and then ended up marrying one of my friends. She didn't rehire me for the second wedding." Melissa thought that even as old as he was—forty?—he looked sad enough to kiss. "My life's work is decomposition. Disasters, abandoned buildings, the occasional crime scene."

In the distance, a car door slammed. Lamar called her name and soon his faded jeans cut through the night like scissor blades. "What the hell's going on? You said you'd be at Florine's, now you're out here with the goddamn photographer?" He had pulled up in the Cordoba after the visitation, asking if he should come by for *the reception*, and when she told him it would only be family and he'd get antsy to leave, he had nodded an affirmative, grinning that he was easy to read.

"We've been talking about vertigo," Melissa said.

"*Vertigo?*" Lamar said. "Can't you just say *fear of heights?*"

"It's not necessarily the same thing," Melissa said.

"You said you'd be at Florine's."

"Lamar, this *is* Florine's. Florine's is right there and my place is right there, and this is Jimmy's *son*, like almost Florine's stepson. We're almost cousins."

"He takes pictures of folks crying around a corpse."

"Lamar, he's a pro who's photographed Katrina and tornado-wrecked towns."

"I'm just a guy who takes pictures. I'm a documentarian."

"I don't care if you're a documentarian, a doctor, or a Doberman pincher," Lamar said. "I don't want you sniffing around my girl."

"Sniffing?" Shane McMurphy said.

"It beats waiting tables, hanging signs, or taking football bets," Melissa said.

"Whose side you on?" Lamar said.

"The side that shows up with grass," Melissa said. Lamar

nodded and looked at the photographer as if to say, *Get that, motherfucker?* He lit a crooked joint and they passed it around. "Lamar works for his uncle at his sign shop. They've got a 125-foot sign that says *SIGNS*. When I was just a girl, I thought that *SIGNS* sign was God's way of telling me that He would show Himself to me. When I grew out of God, I thought it was like a fortune cookie in the sky, and when I happened to see it, I'd search the rest of the day for a message, though the messages never amounted to much. My real fortune cookies always suck. I once had one that said *Why me?*"

"Wasn't that at the Mongoloid Buffet?"

"*Mongolian* Buffett, Lamar," Melissa said. She smiled at the photographer. "See why I ask *Why me?*"

"Why me?" Lamar said, "I'll tell you *why you*. It's because you trust your fate to fortune cookies."

"Maybe *Why me?* is the only question worth asking," Shane McMurphy said. "I imagine that it's the first question that man asked God. It's the darkest and strangest of all paradoxes, perhaps even a hopeful question of identity more than a cynic's question."

"I never once thought of *Why me?* as a hopeful question," Melissa said.

Lamar flicked the roach into the water. He put his finger to Shane's chest. "You, sir, have been sniffing too much formaldehyde." Lamar winked at Shane as if it was all in good fun, and Shane cracked a fearful smile.

Melissa said, "I've always been a bit embarrassed that I asked the question at all. I mean it's like saying that I might have been somebody *if only*."

"And you're sensible enough, baby, to know that just isn't the case," Lamar said.

"Just what the fuck is that supposed to mean?" she said.

Lamar shrugged and handed the photographer one of his *Buck of the Odds* cards, encouraging him to check out the weekend's basketball games.

Later, Melissa lay in bed by herself. *Why me?* she thought—why the *Buck of the Odds?* She listened as the insect songs quieted and rose, got louder and louder, until eventually it felt like some great thing would lift from the ground, shudder and collapse.

The next day, Melissa, wearing a black hat-n-veil at Chloris's request, walked into the funeral home for the memorial service, London and Paris each holding one of her hands. Maynard stood at the door and handed her a program. Doling out sticks of gum to the twins, he said, "London and Paris, you sit quiet and listen to your momma during the service." He held out the pack of gum, like a peace offering, to Melissa.

"I can manage, Maynard," she said.

"Remember, boys, if Granma is to reach heaven, you need to pray for her."

"Otherwise, Momma," Paris said, "she goes to *hail.*"

"Limbo," London said.

"Momma, it's like a time-out from God."

Your father doesn't know where Granma is," Melissa said. "Besides, Granma was Christian, not Catholic. Christians don't go to Limbo, they go…" She took their hands and they stared up at her, waiting and wanting. She released their hands and they took off running, weaving in and out of the mourners like a shadow playing a game of hide-n-seek with itself. "Maynard, just because you sit in church, drink wine and eat crackers, doesn't make you an expert."

"I've got nothing to be ashamed of, Melissa, which is more than I can say for you." He walked away, shaking hands and nodding like he understood it all. She wondered if he knew about Lamar, and if he did, why he couldn't allow her a meager victory by just saying Lamar's name? She turned around to shake the thought, only to catch a quick and big-eyed stare from Barbara, who turned her hunchback away, as if she knew the circumstances of Chloris's final breath. Suddenly, Melissa felt like all eyes were on her, her shame visible like the word on Lamar's naked chest. She was saved when the organist played Glen Campbell's "Arkansas" and folks found their seats. In a whisper, Melissa sang, "Oh how I hated to say goodbye to Arkansas."

Florine read the eulogy, words Chloris wrote, and though Melissa and Florine had joked that they might laugh, when Florine smiled right at her, Melissa found that she didn't have a laugh within her. The twins sat on either side of her, the same dark circles beneath their eyes as those on Maynard. Without even looking at each other, they began to whisper, and when she looked down to hush them, she couldn't tell London from Paris.

That night, after they helped Jimmy and Florine clean up green bean casseroles, deviled eggs, pickled tomatoes, and pound cakes, Melissa and Shane drank vodka from his flask and beer left over from Jimmy's Styrofoam cooler. The boys were asleep in their bedroom, and Shane showed her the digital photographs that he had taken inside the fire-ravaged trailer—images of melted knick-knacks, stick-figure lamps, a mice-infested couch, toy soldiers, and a rotted teddy bear. She took guilty relief in the sensation of walking through the detritus and decay of someone else's life. In the photographs, light poured in from various gaping holes in the roof, budded branches snuck in, ceiling tiles hung like torn, waterlogged skin. A lower denture sat lonely on the kitchen counter. "We lived there first," Melissa said. "Just me and Mamma. Granma sold the trailer after Mamma was sent to Cummins."

"Should I ask?" he said.

"Probably not, but since you're feeding me Smirnoff, I'll tell you that she was sleeping with another woman's husband and he made promises that he didn't keep. She told the jury that she didn't know the woman was pregnant."

"Where's your father?" he said. He traced the outline of the fortune-cookie paper taped to the coffee table. *Why me?*

She felt drunk and reckless, knowing that only things she might regret later would make her feel better now. "What, you think I'll sleep with you if you know me better?"

"We're almost cousins and here we are in Arkansas."

"Funny, you are. When I was a kid, I told everyone that my parents died in a plane accident."

They kissed, and she let his hands explore, wondering if in all his years as a chronic stranger he had photographed a disaster quite like her. Soon they were a tangle of moist mouths and groping hands, most of their clothes still on, her skirt on the floor. When she was at the edge, she pushed up his shirt and bit his shoulder until she drew blood. His arms shuddered, as if he had a chill, and then she was thinking of Chloris, of pressing the pillow into the old woman's face and the body struggling, though she was certain that Chloris had pleaded for that very thing.

When they were done, he said, "Would you believe that like you I was the one who found my grandmother when she died?" Melissa shrugged. She wasn't sure why she should care, but he went on, as if to make some vital point. "I talked to Chloris a number of times. She seemed to think you and I might hit it off."

"Is that why you're here?"

"Partly," he said. "You come with strong recommendations."

"I think that's sicker than funeral photography. Like I told her, she was crazy."

"I don't see it that way," he said. "Maybe Lamar is right. You need to stop asking yourself *Why me?* and just get on with it."

"When you found your grandmother, was it after you held a pillow to her face?" He didn't answer, but he waited, ready for her to unload. "She asked me for mercy and so I did it." Now the tears came and she huddled her knees to her chest, her face between her legs. Shane offered an awkward embrace. They didn't bother to speak, and she didn't bother to move when she heard the Cordoba.

There was a quick knock on the door and then Lamar Asa Hodges stood in front of them.

"Will you look at this," Lamar said. "What in the hell?"

"Lamar, this isn't what you think. I'm just upset is all."

"Upset? Shit, what am I for? But the better question is what in the hell you are doing in your goddamn underwear sitting on this old faggot's lap?" Shane's camera sat on the floor and Lamar picked it up. He turned it over in his hand, puzzling for the button to examine the pictures. When he couldn't find it, he said, "I'll put this shit on the Internet, bitch."

"Come on now," Shane said. "There's nothing going on here, and I do believe she asked you to leave."

Melissa snorted a laugh, unable to believe that such fools surrounded her. Lamar removed the camera's lens cap and lifted it over his head. Shane stood in protest and Lamar tossed the camera, facedown, on the coffee table, shattering the glass top and the lens. Shane leaned for the camera and Lamar met him with an uppercut square in the forehead, sending him into the embrace of the couch. Melissa shouted and Lamar shook his fist in pain.

The twins appeared at the end of hallway. "Get back to bed!" Melissa said.

"Little Maynard and other Little Maynard, come on out! See the saddle tramp you got for a mother!" Shane stood, his index finger at the ready to accuse. Lamar struck two quick blows and Shane's nose exploded in blood and he again collapsed on the couch. Lamar said, "Did she tell you that she comes from a long line of cheating, murdering whores?"

Shane cupped his hand under his nose, his white shirt bloody. "As I understand, her parents died in a plane crash."

Melissa felt herself smiling at the photographer, thinking it might have been the nicest thing anyone had ever said about her.

Lamar was quick to snap her out of whatever pleasant feeling had washed over her.

"I don't get you," Lamar said. "I loved you and this is how you treat me?"

"You ever hear of the Monty Hall Problem, Lamar? This is what we call changing the choice. The chances are better this way. It's called a veridical paradox."

Lamar raised his hand and Shane wheezed and began to push himself up from the couch, which sent Lamar to shaking his head. "Don't worry, buddy, you're the big winner tonight. I'm done beating on your mug, and you're welcome to *that*." He was already walking out the door and without looking back said, "No wonder everything you touch turns to shit."

The boys fished off their island, and through binoculars Melissa watched herons, egrets, and crows. London started crying about a fish that ate half his worm but didn't take the hook, and Paris pointed to the horizon where smoke was rising slow and steady. "Trash, Momma!" One by one, the pillars of smoke rose around Lake Conway, and she thought of Lamar. Soon they looked like the points of some dying star, each set to burning for her. Melissa strained to hear the Cordoba but the only sound was an insect and amphibian buzz that threatened to drown out all her thoughts.

Soon, Maynard floated their way, and the boys set their poles on Y-shaped sticks, running and jumping for their father's attention. But like their great-grandmother had taught them, they hollered, "No trespassing! No fishing! No hunting! That means you!"

"Isn't that the strangest thing?" Maynard said. He pointed out to the fires. "It can't all be trash, can it?"

"Maynard, I'm sure if we tried, we'd find some kind of explanation."

"I know it's a hard time for you, but the kinds of pictures you let that photographer take of you is all over town."

"What?" She wanted to kill Lamar, the dirty Hodges that he was.

"And London and Paris right there in the trailer. Joint custody is what I'm thinking, for the boys' sake."

"Maynard, you can barely make yourself macaroni and cheese. How the hell would you do half-time with the boys?"

"You used to be a respectable woman, Melissa. I'm not so sure anymore."

"Go write another check to the Ukraine."

"Laugh all you want, but for your information, smart ass, the Ukraine is bordered by Russia, Poland, Romania, Hungary, Belarus, Slovakia, and Moldova. She's been swimming in the Black Sea and she's a decent Catholic woman."

"Look, Mamma!" London said. Melissa turned to see the gutted trailer on fire, once again. Tires spun on gravel and she heard the purr of the Cordoba. Sirens sounded in every direction.

Like a lot of folks that early evening in Lake Conway, Melissa and Shane watched the TV news featuring Lamar Asa Hodges' capture by local authorities. Like a man with a plan, Lamar in his 1976 Chrysler Cordoba eluded until he was certain that the media was present for his capture. When the authorities caught Lamar, they treated him kindly—the way cops have always treated Hodges'. They even let Lamar say a few words for the cameras. He uttered her name with nothing but love in his voice, and then he opened his shirt to reveal the inked word: *SHAME.* He said her name again, nothing but malice in his voice.

She threw the remote control against the wall and shouted every obscenity she had ever heard Chloris use to damn the Hodges'. It was then that Shane McMurphy gave her a black-and-white photograph of herself, the twins, Florine and Jimmy, Rose Dawn's clan, Chloris's ashes at their feet. At the bottom of the photograph, as if rising from the top of the urn, was a white light that looked somewhat like a crow, somewhat like the white bandages that now crossed Shane's nose. "What else could it be but a spirit crow, Chloris herself?" he said, claiming innocence, and though she suspected that he doctored the image, it made no difference—it was the kind of lie she was willing to believe.

Weeks later, the sun was setting, the clouds were at a pre-storm boil, and Melissa carted a bucket of ashes, grabbing handfuls and tossing them on the lawn. Shane appeared, and she looked at him as he pressed the shutter. He had been reminding her daily that he should head back to Denver. He had teased her, asking her to leave with him, but then reneging, claiming that he knew her fear of heights would keep her out of Colorado. She wasn't sure that there was much to keep her on Lake Conway.

Melissa tossed ashes in the lake, lamely trying to convince herself that it wouldn't matter when he left. London and Paris, who were supposed to be in the bath, stuck their heads out of the trailer door. Lightning filled the sky and oversized raindrops began to fall. The boys ran to her—London with a bar of soap in his hand—and they began to dance around her. London and Paris were naked, hysterical, but clean, clean, clean.

And like that there was one crow after another, all over the yard, cawing and making a fuss, the photographer catching it all on film. Her legs started to tingle, like water-hungry roots, and she dropped to her knees. The boys kept running in circles. She reached her arms out like branches, the boys circling, slapping her hands and laughing. She liked this feeling, her eyes at the twins' level, the photographer capturing some moment of grace so close to the lake, and she knew that she going nowhere. She didn't know what to name such a lovely feeling, but she thought that she might call it mercy.

THESE ARE MY ARMS

ONE MORNING JEREMY VON MINOR'S WIFE was instructing him on the mysteries of soap making, when the phone rang. It was an irate Madelyn Fischer, who complained that her son, James, was watching pornography for Jeremy's English class. "Don't get me wrong," Madelyn said. "I know the filth playing at every movie theater in town, and how they let kids of any age into those movies, and don't get me started on the Internet. But is it necessary to assign the crap, especially when we're shelling out countless thousands a year for a private school?"

"Mrs. Fischer. Madelyn, I think we first need to consider—"

"Jeremy, I know you're only trying to foster James' interest in film, but why not assign a classic, like *Gone with the Wind* or *Forrest Gump?*"

"The assignment was to read *A Clockwork* Orange, not to watch it."

"Does it make a difference?" Madelyn said. "The movie glorifies sex and violence, not to mention drugs."

Following Darla's instructions, Jeremy sank a saucepan, half-filled with small glycerin cubes, into boiling water. His wife informed him that they were double boiling.

"Filth is filth. Porn is porn, even at high-speed with Beethoven in the background," Madelyn said.

"So…you watched it with him?" Jeremy said.

He heard the *click* of Madelyn hanging up the phone, and he imagined the sound as a detonation, a nitroglycerin device signaled to explode.

Darla said to stir the melting cubes. Four-year-old Orleans

tugged at Jeremy's pant leg and stuck a life-sized, plastic cockroach in her mouth. "Let me see, Dad," she said, the roach wedged between her cheek and gum. She wore a blue wig. Recently, Orleans had been demanding a sister that she would name Lucybelle. She would wear the wig until her parents produced said sibling. Jeremy suspected Darla's parents had given their granddaughter the idea for the protest wig, though when he pressed Orleans, she claimed to have just found it, uncertain of where. To no avail, Darla and Jeremy found themselves frequently explaining how a single child suited them.

"Can I stick the bug in now, Dad?"

"Not yet," Darla said. "Wait until the soap is in the molds."

Ten cubic molds sat on the kitchen counter, though Jeremy had no idea where to begin with any of this soap-making business. Raised by parents who were rock stars turned organic farmers, Darla knew a thing or two about crafts. She was a documentary filmmaker, and as a former student of Nat Mota High School where Jeremy taught, she had lobbied to do a filmmaking workshop for his students.

Jeremy stirred the liquefying substance. "James' mother is pissed because he's watching *A Clockwork Orange*. He's supposed to be reading Anthony Burgess's book, not watching the Kubrick film." He paused from his stirring. "I could blame you."

"You think I have such sway over a teenage boy?" Darla said.

"Mothers are kind of a thing these days," Jeremy said.

"Oh, please," she said, smiling. At thirty-five, Darla's freckled skin was tan from playground and garden sun, her muscles taut from daily yoga, and her ash-blonde hair somewhat brittle from years of home dye jobs. During the film workshops, they had screened her short film *Music Box*, a reflection on the first nine years of her life that were primarily spent on tour with her parents' band The Wound Tights. Her mother had always encouraged her to play with Super-8 and video cameras, and it was this footage that she filmed, a world seen with a child's eyes. Over this was a voiceover that reimagined fairy tales and myths, and Darla reasoned that the film was a complicated response to an unruly upbringing, not that she would have had it any other way.

Now, in the kitchen, the Von Minor family danced to The Wound Tights and after a few hip-shakes and a series of air-guitar windmills, Jeremy poured the melted glycerin into the molds. Orleans stood on a stepstool, talking at a pile of plastic bugs and animals. She dropped in Mr. Cockroach, Miss Dog, Señor Cat, Baby Grasshopper, a fly, and one plastic ring she had hidden in her pocket. Orleans poked at the hot liquid soap. "Ouch!" The clear gel stuck to her fingers.

"Jeremy, keep her away from the soap, please," Darla said, her hands deep in a sinkful of suds and dishes.

"Yeah, Jeremy, keep away from the soap," Orleans mimicked.

He gently pinned her to the kitchen floor. "Tickle torture," he whispered into her blue wig. She squealed. He poked and pinched Orleans; she squirmed and fought, laughed and screamed. He thought Orleans' face an ever-changing mask that was still her, always Orleans. A burst of light froze them. Darla smiled behind a camera.

The phone rang. Jeremy answered. It was James. He apologized for his mother, said the movie was "eggiweggy, droog." Now that James had begun talking like the characters in the movie, Jeremy was positive that he would never read the book. The students at Nat Mota High School were *at-risk*; you could ask them. But they weren't necessarily underprivileged. James' father was vice-president of product development for national pet food company Land O' Chow, and when the weather turned colder, a mealy smell oozed from the dog food plant and seeped into Denver.

After Darla's filmmaking workshop, James decided that he would make his own personal documentary, an auto-biopic of a sort. *A Clockwork Orange* gave him some good ideas. Jeremy told him to read the book, to do the assignment. James said, sounding too much like one of the English hoodlums from the movie, "Just doing some preliminary research, my brother." He cleared his throat and then whispered, "You know those wolf masks in Sonja's class? They would be perfect for a little something in my film. As you know, I'm doing my best to stay out of trouble, and I was wondering if perhaps you could secure them for me."

"Out of the question," Jeremy said.

"You'd be doing me a solid and help to keep me from straying from the path of righteousness. I've got a serious artistic need for those canine masks."

"Goodbye," Jeremy said.

The Von Minors walked out onto the front deck while the soap molds set. To the west, the Rockies baked in the early autumn sun. On the high plains, Sloan's Lake simmered and shimmered. A neighbor washed her car, and her portable radio played a public radio station reporting the statistical data on wars and weather, surveys and stocks. On the eastern horizon, Denver's skyline stretched one mile from the lake. When the air was clean, the skyline was a crisp series of building-block right angles. This day, however, was a Red Day, which meant bad air quality and haze, and a myopic view of the city. During the summer, Red Days occurred infrequently. Blue Days were clean days. A fire had just been contained outside Boulder, and the microscopic residue of smoke still lingered. Nearly twenty weather stations monitored the air that the citizens breathed and the ozone that filtered the violent rays of the sun. There was good ozone and bad ozone, but how to tell the difference? Jeremy knew that the weather stations tested for carbon monoxide, sulfur dioxide, nitric oxide, and nitrogen dioxide, as well as 10-micron particulates and 2.5-micron particulates. These figures were posted online each morning. Jeremy didn't know what any of them meant, but he knew Blue from Red. Homeland Security Presidential Directive-3 had declared that today was a Yellow Day. Each morning, he checked the air quality and the threat of terror. Two years ago, he had taught Orleans her colors through these daily-posted codes.

Jeremy knew firsthand that most parents existed in varying states of fear. He and Darla were no different, though they mostly feared the fear and, of course, the fearful. Asthma, ADD, OCD, school phobia, hyperactivity, laziness, genius—the kids at Nat Mota had them all. The students' parents interchangeably labeled and diagnosed. The two were the same as far as they were concerned. Gifted and talented, brain, athlete, obese, anorexic, bulimic, hyper, aggressive, passive-aggressive, passive-gifted, obese-talented, anorexic-impulsive. Labeling helped the parents quantify and qualify their failures and celebrate and publicize their successes.

Jeremy watched while Orleans continued to blow bubbles. Each bubble a sphere, each sphere a world that she gleefully popped. He wondered how afraid he was for her future. Was he afraid at all? He didn't think that he was, but he considered the fact that this might make him a bad parent. All good parents were concerned parents, and anyone who paid any attention at all to the world around them was afraid. Weren't they? Hadn't Jeremy heard that if you weren't afraid, the terrorists had already won, or was it the other way around? Jeremy knew many people whose fear fueled their patriotism; their fear replaced their patriotism.

Fear was the new patriotism.

As per their Friday-night date ritual, Jeremy and Darla Von Minor hired a babysitter and in a Mayan-inspired theater with deco sensibilities watched a re-run of *The Filth and the Fury*, a film that chronicled the Sex Pistols and their fall from angst-filled grace.

After the movie they sat talking in the car. "So much style wasted," Jeremy said.

"It's hard to stay pissed off though," Darla said. "Isn't that why we retreat and raise families?"

"Last night," Jeremy said, "a pollster called about the war and asked me if I was very angry, moderately angry, or slightly angry with the President's policies, and of course I said, 'Very angry.' The pollster thanked me and I hung up, but when I got to thinking about it, I wasn't all that angry anymore, and I began to wonder if maybe opinion polls are cathartic."

"Opinion polls are the opiate of the self-satisfied," Darla said.

When they had first started dating five years before, Jeremy had feigned an interest in Darla's political concerns, what he referred to as her *body politic*. At one time, Darla had been married to an activist. The day after their wedding, the spirits of the forest had called her husband to tree-sit in protest of logging down in Sandbench. Though Darla sympathized with his calling, the marriage, a subject of another of her documentary films, was soon annulled. Darla and Jeremy began to sleep together. Darla was at a Labor march when a fight broke out between a woman wearing leather pants and a PETA member armed with a red-dye-filled squirt gun. A riot ensued. Wearing a Nixon mask, Darla had been one of many marching up Colfax Avenue, and she was the first to receive a whack from a cop's billy club. Days after her release from the hospital she was still vomiting, attributing it to a concussion. A week later, Darla discovered that the nausea was not caused by the cop's club, and seven months after that the midwife said, "It's a girl!" The recently married couple named her Orleans.

Cool breezes fell from the Rockies, mixing with warm asphalt, steel, and concrete to create an inner-city climate that throbbed with each gust of wind. In the theater parking lot on South Broadway, Jeremy and Darla sat in their all-wheel-drive station wagon, windows rolled down, and observed patrons sliding in and out of Kitty's XXX, where one could purchase novelties and movies, or watch porn in coin-operated privacy.

They watched a man exit, and Darla said, "He's got four kids."

"And an overweight wife who wears her pajamas well past lunchtime," Jeremy said.

"Sometimes I wear my pajamas well into the afternoon."

"You're active. This woman watches game shows and compulsively eats Hot Pockets. Pitiful, yes, but she's a nervous soul and awaits anxiously her husband's return from work."

"So her husband," Darla mused, "what's with him? In this age of virtual privacy and virtual community, why does he seek release in a sex shop? Is he brave or depraved?"

"There's the thrill of public humiliation?"

Darla tuned in to the college radio station and they listened to a man singing about high fashion during wartime. "Let's not forget the public's need for exposure of any kind," she said. "That man made a serious political statement by leaving his wife's side and masturbating in front of a television screen within the confines of what amounts to a broom closet."

"Do you think he's lonely, that the theater is his prison?"

Jeremy didn't feel lonely, though he sometimes felt ineffectual. He often found himself both admiring and hating those who were successful, never trusting their motivations or intentions. "We've been conned into believing that we must go public with everything," he said.

"The sign post of our age is the sign post," Darla said. "We map our identities with logos, brands, and on computer sites. If you don't identify yourself, the community will do it for you. That man just exposed the fact that he's in hiding."

"He's announcing to the world that he's entering the closet."

"We're nothing without our closets." Neon streetlight bathed Darla's face and hands, and pink-flushed clouds pressed down from the sky.

"So what's your closet?" Jeremy said.

"Hah! I can't tell you. I've got a mansion of closets. I'd be nothing without them."

Jeremy knew this to be true, that they were one of those couples who would not bare their respective histories, though he often insisted that he had nothing to hide. He had no particular big and dark secrets, more like an endless trickle of failures, indiscretions, and humiliations.

He pointed to a woman wearing sweat pants, a shape-hugging T-shirt, and a Broncos cap snug over her too-short hair. "That's Madelyn Fischer, James' mother," Jeremy said. They watched her enter Kitty's.

"She's a porn-consuming hypocrite," Darla said. "You should totally get those masks for James. He's under a tyrant's rule."

Jeremy thought about this for a moment. He considered requesting permission for James to use the masks in his film project, but he was afraid of the questions that Donald Mota might ask, inquiries into content, form, objectives. Jeremy didn't have the answers. Asking Donald for permission meant exposing his own apathy and ineptness. He did want James to express himself, so he decided to give James his trust, somewhat in the manner that Siegfried and Roy must have once submitted faith to untrained tigers. Jeremy put the car in gear and they drove to Nat Mota High School.

Alone in the pitch dark of Sonja's history classroom, Jeremy felt his way around the rows of desks. In his haste, he had neglected to bring a flashlight. Maps charting the shifting global-political lines of the last two centuries covered his colleague's walls, but in the dark, they were prehistoric landmasses. He stood atop a desk, leaning out over the mantle of a tiled fireplace, groping the wall for a fur-covered canine mask. He found purchase on the mask, hooked a finger into each of the eye sockets, and pulled from the wall. Jeremy choked on two decades worth of dust and reached for the second mask, but he coughed too hard while leaning too far. The desk shifted and he toppled, his cheek smacking against another desk. Cursing under his breath, he held the mask aloft, as if it were a puppet, its blank eyes searching the room for danger. Jeremy listened for approaching footsteps, touched a finger to his cheek, put the finger to his tongue, and tasted blood. When he regained his composure, he retrieved the second mask and realigned the disturbed classroom furniture.

Back at the car, Jeremy collapsed in the driver's seat.

"Maybe you just constructed a closet, dear."

"A shoebox, at most," he said.

"My renegade coward," she said.

After sending the babysitter home and checking on Orleans, Jeremy and Darla stood in front of the mirrors above his-and-her sinks, Darla dabbing a washcloth to Jeremy's cheek. "You're like a cat burglar, Jeremy Von Minor," she said. "Meow."

"Funny, I don't feel too cat-like."

"You're supposed to land on your feet. Anyway, it's just a scrape." Jeremy pulled the masks from the bag. The snouts were intact, the eye sockets empty, beads and leather tassels hanging from the ears like canine braids. Darla held up, at arm's-length, one of the masks. "Bow-wow," she said, with a grimace on her face.

Jeremy sat in an overstuffed armchair and Donald Mota sat on the opposite side of the desk, running an ivory letter opener along his jaw. "So what's this about you assigning dirty movies?" Donald said. Donald exclusively wore khaki pants and shirts, a silk ascot added for formal occasions; he looked like a political tyrant crossed with an animal trainer, which, as he saw it, perfectly fit his job description. Jeremy explained that he had assigned James a book report of his own choosing, not a movie. Donald said that Jeremy should have *assigned a specific text*, and furthermore, all texts needed to be cleared through him. This was the reason Jeremy never cleared anything.

The mounted heads of large animals, mostly from Southern

Africa, where Donald used to go big-game hunting, lined the walls of his office. Nat Mota, Donald's father, had been a safari guide who taught English to villagers and tribes in the Southern Hemisphere. When he returned to America, Nat Mota purchased large tracts of ranch land on the Colorado high plains and the adjoining Front Range. In Denver, Nat Mota purchased a sandstone mansion and opened Mountain View Asylum, *My bughouse*, he would call it among friends. The Motas bounced between the bughouse and the ranch house and summered in safari tents. When Nat passed on in 1969, Donald, thirty-one and philanthropic, renovated the bughouse into a schoolhouse for disgruntled youth.

The classroom where Jeremy taught had four elk heads, all shot by students—students Donald had taken on hunting trips back in the early seventies. Jeremy's students called them *The Four Elk of the Apocalypse*. Donald referred to the students as *feral youth*.

Of course, these days Nat Mota High School didn't sponsor armed hunting trips. Afternoons at Nat Mota were spent 'in the field,' and so Jeremy arranged daily field trips for his advisees, who typically had an interest in English and the arts. Darla had suggested that this year his class focus on the Arts & Social Change. This had come on the heels of Donald choosing The Winning of the West. Jeremy escorted the students to museums. They hiked Mount Evans, painted each other's portraits, and explored the simulacra of the Manitou Cliff Dwellings. Jeremy attempted to counteract his students' suburban upbringings, and as Nat Mota had tried to civilize the so-called *primitive people*, Jeremy did his best to enlighten the *consumer-savage*.

"By the way, Jeremy, two Wazoo masks are missing from Sonja's room. I shot those canines at the lip of Eldorado Canyon. My great-grandmother sewed the headdresses in sixty-three."

"A Wazoo mask?" Jeremy said.

"Wazoo Indians, which I happen to be the last of. My brother and my children long since forfeited their Wazoo legacy."

"Don't take this the wrong way, Donald, but I've never heard of the Wazoo, well except for when people say 'up the wazoo.'"

"Are you calling me an asshole?"

"Why no, I—"

Donald chuckled. "Just kidding, my boy. Wazoo, Wazee, Wahoo, who knows?" His tone grew somber. "Time bends language, Jeremy. Time writes new rules for the ancients. We call this power to change the past 'living history.' They couldn't spell for a damn, but the Wazoos were a proud people. I need those masks back." Donald examined the letter opener. "Keep your ears open. They'll talk."

"The masks?"

"Would you prefer that I just gave the keys to the students, let them have reign?" Donald sighted the ivory letter opener on Jeremy's cheek. "Not to pry, but did you get into a fight or something?"

"Bicycle accident," Jeremy lied.

Jeremy walked across the campus, which encompassed a city block upon a hill that overlooked a lake, an interstate, and the frontline of the Rocky Mountains. It was a Blue Day, not a cloud in the sky, and he braced himself against the vapors of early morning teenage lethargy. When his homeroom advisees arrived, they brought with them the smells of a crisp morning mixed with cigarette and marijuana smoke, flowery perfumes, fruity hair gels, breakfast cereal, and chocolate milk.

Every morning in Jeremy's homeroom the kids left wordplay that they called *cryptos* on the chalkboard. They liked to gut words and leave them sprawled out like carcasses. That day the board read: *O penmanship open man's hip.* Jeremy suspected that a form of primitive committee created and tested the cryptos. Their anonymity gave Jeremy a fuzzy feeling of satisfaction, as if something he had done as a teacher had caused his students to become secret admirers of language itself.

Later, at 1:30 in the afternoon, Jeremy sat in the fifteen-seat van, waiting, while across the street his students stood on the sidewalk finishing their cigarettes. These kids wore big pants and visible underwear, raver bellbottoms, safety-pinned shirts, cocked baseball caps, and black fingernails—they were nerd chic, gangster-poser, skinhead, skinny punk, post-Dead hippie, and revisionist prepster.

"Let's go," Jeremy said. Grumbles, mumbles, disregard. They filed into the van. James, a senior, sat up front with Jeremy, and his partner in crime, Dolly, sat on the bench behind them.

"Jeremy, you see Dolly's new tat?" James said. Jeremy had noticed the tattoo in third period, sophomore English, but Dolly stuck her foot up on his armrest anyway. She traced the red-and-black devil and its long tail, which wrapped all the way around her ankle and shined with petroleum jelly. "This is my leg," she said.

"Don't you have to be eighteen to get a tattoo?" he said.

The van was awash in conspiracy theories, and Jeremy listened attentively.

"It's a false contract. Lawmakers are under the assumption that we agree to laws just because we're born in a certain region of the globe."

"If you think about it, it certainly is. Lawmakers and law enforcers are only a subculture of a vast network of cultures, and everyone is under the assumption that we've agreed to their laws."

"I've agreed to nothing."

"Lawmakers were those kids who were always modifying and changing rules while a game was already in progress. We called them cheaters then. I call them cheaters now."

"Is this everyone?" Jeremy interrupted.

They all looked around, as if they didn't recognize one another. "Wait, here comes Easton!" The boy bustling toward the van looked like a runaway scarecrow wearing a backpack. The first four years of his life, he and his family had lived in a cult compound that was burned to the ground by federal agents, and whenever Jeremy saw the kid running to the van, he couldn't help but think about him running to escape flames.

Blond hair and rail thin, Easton waved. "I'm coming!" he said. James snapped a Polaroid. Easton plopped into the vacant spot next to Dolly, who still had her tattoo up for inspection. Easton slid the door shut and they all breathed the same tepid air. From the back of the van someone growled, someone else barked.

James handed Easton the yet-to-develop Polaroid. Easton said thanks, fanned the photo paper, and watched as his own worried face materialized. Every day Easton was late for the van, James took a photograph and Easton kept this collection behind the clear plastic of his binder. Easton was going to sell them on E-Bay when James became famous

They settled in and prepared for travel. Jeremy buckled and then turned to ask if they had, too; a requirement of the job. They held the male and female parts in their hands and moved them together, like clumsy, drunken lovers. Metal and plastic clanked but nothing was inserted. They had been raised with child seats, bicycle helmets and knee pads, but bodily safety was the last of their concerns.

"So, do you like it, Jeremy?" Dolly said. She flourished her hand over her ankle as if displaying merchandise. Beneath her black beanie, her green eyes were honest and wanting. Dolly Byrd's mother called the school at least three times a week. The Byrd household throbbed with tension. Fights, absent nights, drugs, threats, all within the gated paradise of Denver's northwest suburbs. Dolly behaved perfectly in his class and really, most of the students did. Against his cynical nature, he sometimes tried to imagine them as transcendent or divine beings. If they were not angels but devils, so be it. He couldn't help but agree with Dolly, who was found of saying, *Devils are the same as angels but just a lot fucking cooler.*

"The conception we have of Satan with a beard, that's not historically accurate," Easton said. He was still breathing hard from his run, and the odor of ranch potato chips hung, almost visible, about him. "The image of Satan with a beard was nothing more than American propaganda against Communism. See, Satan looks like Lenin."

Jeremy couldn't take his eyes from the shiny devil. "Go ahead," Dolly said. Jeremy put a finger to the petroleum-slick black beard. It occurred to Jeremy that he had never touched a tattoo that fresh. He wrapped his hand around her ankle and easily touched his middle finger to his thumb. "Oh, glorious Satan," he said in some vague European accent. Easton tickled Dolly, who bucked forward, Jeremy's hand now on a meaty portion of her denim-cutoff-covered thigh. Dolly, blushing, slapped at Easton. Jeremy, blushing, turned and started the van. James reviewed the footage he had just captured on his phone.

At the Denver Public Library, they each compiled research for a term paper on this year's theme. As they entered, a security guard spoke into her walkie-talkie, no doubt putting the other officers on heightened alert. *Orange* to *Red.* James touched Jeremy's shoulder and pointed out all of the video cameras. "Never forget that you're always being filmed," James said.

The students' approaches to the umbrella topic of Arts & Social Change had required some fine-tuning, including, Jeremy thought, figuring out how it connected to the theme. Dolly had expressed interest in an acting career, but then she reasoned that her short stature limited her options, so she would choose either news anchor or porn star, no anal. She had recently eliminated news anchor. Though Jeremy had no desire to see Dolly chase the KY-covered carrot of porn stardom, he could not strip her of her ambitions, thus, he would help her understand the operation of bodily presentation. He encouraged her to study marginal performance art, freak shows, and, of course, the history, people, and effects of the porn industry itself. Jeremy hoped that as she cloaked the *idea* of porn star with layer upon layer of academic gobbledygook, pornography's allure would be lost. He had vetoed a series of Dolly's working titles, including "Makin' Money While Makin' Love," "Fallacies of Filmed Fornication," and "Coitus Interruptus: Let's Stop and Think About Pornography." She had settled on "The Revolutionary Body."

But what troubled Jeremy was that she had recently been rumored to be James' acting talent.

That night as they made love, Darla said, "Do you ever picture me as anyone else when we have sex?" The arched ceiling refracted and amplified sound; sometimes it seemed to Jeremy that Darla's questions came from the outer reaches of the future, perhaps some corner in her mansion of closets.

"Never," Jeremy lied. "Why? Do you picture me as someone else?"

"Sometimes, but I don't imagine you as a person. I see you as a natural disaster, a mountain crumbling, an earthquake or a flood."

Jeremy made a joke about the Wonder Twins, a cartoon he remembered from childhood: "Wonder Twin powers, activate— form of a wolf, shape of an avalanche."

When there was nothing left of them but heavy breathing, Jeremy touched her stretch marks. He pulled back the covers and by candlelight examined the grooves in her skin, wrinkles and waves of time. "It's like glaciers ran the length of your hips." She rolled her eyes and dragged her nails up the length of his arms. "Sometimes it makes me sad that our little girl's name is now equated with disaster and the failure of public officials."

They named her Orleans Louise after the city where they spent their honeymoon. They were poor—newlyweds, a nervous, drunken groom and an obviously pregnant bride. After the recent Hurricane Katrina, Orleans' name seemed like an ominous choice. But Orleans was healthy, funny, and wise; she had outgrown her flood-prone stage; she was not a victim, not a product of federal and local negligence. She had never looted or been looted. Darla's father had once joked that with Darla and Jeremy for parents, Orleans, unlike New Orleans, was sufficiently dammed.

Today, a Blue Day, they would see an exhibit of Allen Ginsberg's photography. Jeremy did not mention this trip. Though in all likelihood Donald would have consented, Jeremy feared the conversation might lead to divulging the content of his "Beat-heavy" literature classes that fall. The Beat writers weren't part of Nat Mota's curriculum, and neither were profane Englishmen like Anthony Burgess, whose *A Clockwork Orange* inspired the film that so perturbed James' mother. Donald believed that violence and colonialism were the impetus of history—a book written in blood—but he insisted that teachers avoid *prurient texts*. Overt confrontation gave Jeremy ulcers, so he resisted in secret, teaching the books that had inspired him, passing them on to his students as if he were Montag in *Fahrenheit 451*.

Images lined the walls—Ginsberg and pals in all their self-aware Beatific glory. The students walked with notebooks in hand, scribbling and pointing. Easton stood in front of a photograph of Neal Cassidy and Timothy Leary. "The bus, the bus, the bus," he said, his voice impatient, as if he might get left behind. In class, they had read *One Flew Over the Cuckoo's Nest*, and on his own Easton read *The Electric Kool-Aid Acid Test*. Now he punctuated exclusively with exclamation points and ellipses. He grabbed his pencil from behind his ear and began his overpunctuated notes.

An elderly couple stood in the far corner and when they made for the exit, Jeremy took advantage of the empty gallery. With his hands behind his back, he circled the small kiosk. "Let's think about counterculture. What, if anything, do the subjects of these photographs seem *counter* to? Do the images add to what we already know, or think we know, about Beat literature? Are we engaging the images as fans, say in the way we look at images of rock stars? Who are these outcasts and outlaws who become icons?" The kids knew the writers and personas in the photographs—Kesey, Kerouac, Burroughs, Cassidy, Ginsberg—and when they weren't familiar with someone, they wanted the lowdown from Jeremy—Corso, Ferlinghetti, Snyder. They had done a Neal Cassidy/Beat tour of Denver—Holy Ghost Church where Cassidy was baptized, 23rd and Welton baseball games, Five Points jazz. They had eaten burgers and greasy onion rings at My Brother's Bar, where an autographed photo of Kerouac and Cassidy greeted you before you walked through the restroom doors. Jeremy pointed to the photo of Timothy Leary. "So many years later, do these writers offer us more than an excuse to turn on, tune in, drop out?"

Out of the corner of his eye, Jeremy watched James pull a tiny digital camera from his pants pocket. From the hip, James snapped a flashless shot. He dropped the camera in his pocket and smiled back at Jeremy, who mouthed the words, "No photos." James pointed to the image of Burroughs—his hero—with a camera in his hands. James made a clipping motion with his fingers, signing what Jeremy assumed was *cut-up*. Short of frisking James, there was really no way to stop him, and anyhow, his pictures made good teaching tools. James, Dolly, and Easton huddled around a Kerouac photograph. It was the image on the front cover of *Desolation Angels*, which Dolly had been carrying around in her backpack. James mocked the pose, hand deep in pocket, forefinger and thumb to lip, a masculine inhale. They all began to chatter in some group frenzy that Jeremy had yet to understand how they pulled off. "Jeremy, let's get some spray paint and drive the van to Frisco... Ain't got no time... go, go, go... I saw the best minds... There he is, Old Bull... Faggot, yes, queer, yes, junkie, yes!... Get in the van!... That's Henry Rollins, jackass!... Grass, lid, Benzedrine... Let's do Larimer Street one more time! Denver! Denver!"

For a moment, he thought he heard a dog whimper. Someone began to quietly yip, and it occurred to Jeremy that something peculiar might be going on with Donald's Wazoo canine masks. Jeremy straightened his tie, walked over to where four students stood around a photograph of a naked Allen Ginsberg dancing on the beach. Easton scratched his head, looked at Jeremy, and said, "Bow-wow."

Jeremy whispered, "Okay, so what's going on with the masks?"

James shrugged, looked truly puzzled, and walked away. Someone whimpered. Jeremy closed his eyes in frustration and confusion. James said Jeremy's name from behind him, and when he turned James snapped a picture. He showed Jeremy the digital screen and there he was, asleep on his feet, Ginsberg's photo-gray testicles hanging above his right shoulder. "No photographs," Jeremy said. It was one of those moments in which he feigned control.

It was a Blue Day and the chalkboard read, *artifice. if art, ice. I'm free! (zing!)*. The kids barked and growled all day.

Later, Jeremy saw Donald in the hallway. "Those Wazoo masks are back safe and sound." Donald winked at Jeremy and said, "Tough love tames the savage beast."

That afternoon, they went to see Body Worlds at the Denver Nature and Science Museum. In the van, James passed around a picture that Paul, a Nat Mota graduate who had joined the military, had sent from The Desert. Paul stood in his skivvies, flexing his muscles. "Paul's ripped, man, oh shit!" someone said.

"Obviously Congress is failing to fund body armor *and* the very basics in clothing," Easton said.

"Supposedly, Easton, you showed more than that in the movie."

"When are we going to see that masterpiece of pornography?" someone said.

Through the rearview, Jeremy saw Dolly blush. "It's not pornography," she said.

"What happened to your career aspirations?" someone else said.

"Nudity does not equal pornography, you asshole."

"James, please tell me that this film is not what they're saying it is," Jeremy said.

"Who cares what butthole critics have to say?" James said. Easton fidgeted in his seat. Dolly chewed her nails.

Jeremy stopped the van and they all piled out.

After waiting in line, they stood before real human bodies plasticized by different artists, some who wanted to offer an anatomical lesson, some who wanted to flay the body and spread its pieces out for identification, and others who wanted to say, *Look what a dead human body can do.* One was called "Exploding Woman" and the effect was like something out of a Dali painting, the symmetrical sections of her body released to the effects of universal entropy. On some, the dried tendons looked like beef jerky gone bad.

Dolly said, "I'd like to donate my body to science."

"You'd most certainly have to be dead," Easton said. They stood next to a woman lying on her side, her pregnant belly holding a plastic baby.

"No," Dolly said. "I'd like to donate my body to science when I'm in my prime."

"The process would certainly kill you then," Easton said. "Imagine being soaked in acetone." He stopped, grabbed Dolly's hand, and examined her chipped and chewed fingernails in the museum light. "Imagine your body frozen and then soaked in fingernail polish remover until all the fat and water in your body—that's almost all of you—is replaced by the remover. Then you're placed in a bath of liquid plastic. Let's say epoxy resins, though it could be polyester or silicone rubber. Then we create a vacuum and all that fingernail polish remover begins to boil and is replaced by the plastic. We cure you like a Virginia ham, but in gas or light or heat." A small crowd had gathered and Easton stood triumphant in his knowledge. "Voilà, you're plasticized."

"I don't want to be plasticized," Dolly said. "It would be like me, and say like criminals who had nothing better to do, and we'd just stand around and people could study human anatomy."

"That's what most people use the Internet for," Easton said.

"Excuse me, sir?" A skinny man with glasses and a goatee leaned toward Easton's ear. "I can get fingernail polish, the resin, and the heat, but how exactly would I create a vacuum?"

"Well, you'd start by—"

Dolly took Easton by the arm and led him away from the would-be plasticine serial killer. "I just don't get it," Dolly said. "Why can't they exhibit live bodies, let people look around, see what a living body is like?"

A plastic swimmer, a winged man, and a man on a horse. On one plastic man, testes hung like Christmas bulbs tied to a human tree, a Christ-like Christmas tree. Jeremy imagined that in the future plastination would be the technique they used to preserve loved ones. The future population would worship preserved ancestral viscera—muscles, tendons, and stomachs—rather than photographs and family genealogy. They would return to the body as the source.

On the ride home, no one sat up front but Jeremy. A mile from the museum, he looked in the rearview mirror and they were all topless—even the girls. "Back on with the clothes, please!" Jeremy quickly looked away. "Put your clothes on, I said."

"On field trips before you've let us hike without shirts," Easton said.

"That was just the—" Jeremy refused to fall into the gender trap. "Put your damn shirts on."

"How is this different?" Easton asked.

Silence pervaded the van and the mood seemed to shift to something darker. The van's tires vibrated against the asphalt skin of the road. No one said a word; no one budged. Jeremy preferred not to look back, not to see whether they were following orders.

When they reached Nat Mota, they piled out of the van,

jackets and pants on each and every one. No one said goodbye, but as each hopped out the door, they left an article of clothing. The mound sat in the passenger seat, and Jeremy was quite uncertain what to do with it.

At home, Orleans and Jeremy sat in front of the full-length mirror in the hallway. They were playing TV show, in particular a show they called *I Love Lucybelle*. Orleans put the blue wig on Jeremy's head and ducked behind him, the top of her rat's nest and eyes visible. "Dance!" she commanded. She moved her father by his elbows as if he were her blue-haired puppet. She let go, and now Jeremy had two full-size arms and two child-size arms. "Dance!" she commanded, as they both moved their arms.

"I am Lucybelle, Shiva of the American suburbs, breather of bad air, destroyer of strip malls, parking lots, and crappy public art," Jeremy said.

"Lucybelle's got four arms," Orleans said.

Jeremy wanted to say *has four arms*, but he was enjoying the moment too much to scold. Darla came up from behind them and made a sandwich with Orleans between them. Now six arms danced. It was simple and pure delight.

One cold Red Day, the chalkboard read, *dog do doog good od god* and Jeremy erased it immediately. Boys flicked their tongues between V-ed fingers at Dolly and the girls shunned her, whispered and laughed. Dolly went home sick after first period. When Jeremy walked outside, he smelled the mealiness of Land O' Chow. It seemed that winter would soon arrive.

The next day, another Red Day, the air was thick with a stench not unlike a moldy grain barrel. During the afternoon, Jeremy raked leaves. Orleans came outside and wanted to help. He told her to bring the garden hose around to the front of the house so he could shoot leaves from the corners of the deck. Orleans was wearing the blue wig but not a jacket. "Get some warm clothes on first," he said.

"Wait!" she said, running back inside. In seconds, she was outside again, spraying the hose. "Don't get wet," he said. He considered telling her not to waste water, but he didn't. Darla opened the front door and said he had a phone call. "I think it's Donald."

"And you, get inside," Darla said.

Orleans looked shocked and then smiled. She still had the hose in her hand and had soaked an oak as high as the water would reach. "What? I'm making leaves grow back." Water dripped from the branches, like her own personal rain shower. She stood in the mist and her grin refused to leave.

"Do you want her to catch pneumonia?" Darla said as Jeremy walked inside.

The call from Donald Mota was interrupted by a call from Madelyn Fischer, which was interrupted by a call from James Fischer. "There's a DVD in your bag," James said. "Watch it, and remember, everything was done voluntarily." James hung up the phone.

Jeremy got back on the line with Donald and they scheduled a meeting the following morning. "Madelyn Fischer called me," Jeremy said. "I need to call her back."

"She's ready to explode. Let me intercede. But tell me what you know about this…this porno ring?" Donald said.

"Are they calling it a porn ring already?"

"No one makes a *single* porno movie. The industry is a virus."

"Have you seen it?" Jeremy said.

"No. You?"

"No, but I wonder if we should watch it."

"Absolutely not! We can't watch a student pornography film. Watching the act implicates the viewer as a sponsor of pornography."

"But if we don't know the contents of the film, its intent—"

"Do you have access to the movie?" Donald asked, his voice slow and tempered.

"It sounds as if it's readily available."

"That girl, Dolly Byrd, she's only fifteen?"

"That's correct," Jeremy said.

"Easton Albion, he's the cult kid, right?"

"Former cult kid."

"Also fifteen."

Jeremy pulled the movie out. The title read *SATIN SATAN SAT AN SAT AN SAT*. It was not unlike his Nat Mota darlings to slip gifts into his bag: photographs (usually of himself); poems: *i'm a rock* written on a stone; a leaf with black magic marker that said *please don't leaf me*. This deposit seemed more like a hex than a gift.

With Orleans confined to her room, Darla and Jeremy put the movie in the DVD player. The opening credits rolled. *SATIN SATAN SAT AN SAT AN SAT starring Byrdy and Alibi. A Dog Gone Good Production.* Photographs changed rapidly across the screen. Babies, kids, parents holding kids, so fast that some were indiscernible.

The photographs stopped and there were the hideous dog masks, covering the heads of a man and a woman, the elasticity of their flesh giving away their youth. They growled. The long strands of hide and fur covered both of the actors' bare chests. *Oh, glorious Satan*, a low, slow voice said.

Darla looked at Jeremy and smiled. "You assigned this?"

"I only assign reading and writing."

Oh, glorious Satan sounded from the television. It was Jeremy's voice, this time at normal speed. "You're a regular Mel Blanc, you are," Darla said.

A concrete wall, maybe a warehouse or a factory. On the wall, red spray paint read: *Land O, c- how?. daddy. d-day. dy dad dy!!!!!* The masked couple growled and sniffed at each other. A close-up of a breast in silhouette, an eggplant, a shrunken scrotum, a sunset, and a building on fire. Sniffing and biting. The couple on all fours on the concrete floor, pawing and prodding, and then the full-frontal nudity that they had been expecting. The masked woman lifted her hands above her head and turned her body to the side. A tattooed devil on the girl's ankle. "That's Dolly."

"You mean *Byrdy.*"

"And Easton."

"*Alibi,*" Darla corrected.

Oh, glorious Satan over and over again, the voice's speed running fast and then slow. Dolly and Easton disappeared under a sheet beneath the table. The sheet moved this way and that, like an epileptic Casper the Ghost, or like two bodies mid-coitus, but somehow the sheet remained fixed on them, over them, hiding their flesh. The photographs started again, slowly moving across the bottom of the screen, like teletype—images of the Nat Mota mansion, a birthday party with pointed hats, The Desert, a preteen pajama party, a wedding-ringed hand wrapped around a tattooed ankle, a dog food factory, the Denver skyline, Jeremy's face, students' faces, Easton running late, back to the dog food factory, oil refineries. The actors sighed and collapsed under the sheet. The camera panned up, rested on a dog food logo (a dog standing on its head), and faded to black.

"Well, it was an ambitious effort, but it wasn't porn," Darla said. "James has a good eye, though too quick, quick, quick for my taste," Darla said, snapping her fingers. "Not exactly a movie for show-and-tell, but some cool shots."

"Really cool shots of a naked fifteen-year-olds."

"What? They see worse on TV!"

"You're kidding, right? These are my students we're talking about. A DVD in my bag?"

The phone rang. Madelyn Fischer said, "I'm going to have your job." Madelyn had spoken with Dolly's mother, who got a call from someone else's father, and "that tape is going to be the end of your teaching days. I recognize your voice and your wedding ring from a parent-teacher conference."

Jeremy felt dizzy with dread, and he was sure she could sense the sweat dripping from his armpits.

"I know for a fact that you have a copy. Evidently, everyone has one."

"I didn't have anything to do with it."

"Do you know that that girl's parents are going to press charges?"

"You think I told them to make that thing? It was filmed at *your* husband's plant."

"I wouldn't know. I didn't get a chance to see it, as you obviously have."

"Oh, God." He hadn't meant to say it aloud.

"I used to think you were good for those kids. I did. You're the first teacher James has ever liked, but we're a Christian family. My husband's already talked to our lawyer and the next call I'm making—"

Jeremy hung up. The light was fading outside and the western horizon—the Rockies—was washed in orange-red hues. Red Days always made for better sunsets, but this one looked like an ulcer. It threatened snow.

"Somebody's here!" Orleans yelled, running out of her room and frantically securing her wig. Jeremy walked to the door, expecting it to be the police, the FBI, or Donald Mota with a safari rifle he'd use to put Jeremy down like a rabid dog. "Go clean your room," Jeremy said. Orleans gave a long, drawn-out *But!* and then skipped away. Jeremy opened the door and James stood there, hands in his pockets, eyes on the porch floorboards.

They went for a walk around the lake. "Your mother called me."

James kept his eyes from Jeremy. Geese beat their wings, large bodies lifting off the ground, but only moving a few feet. Their white necks absorbed the ulcerated light, as if they were blushing.

"It wasn't meant to be released. The movie was a draft, a runaway draft."

"A runaway draft? You made the thing for people to watch. What were you thinking?" It was getting colder by the second. The snow started to fall in big flakes.

"Dolly's parents...I think the cops will be at my house if I go back."

"If she were my daughter, I'd be kicking your ass right now."

"My father has lawyers."

"I didn't say that I *am* going to kick—"

"I'm not worried about the cops, I mean. Dolly makes her own choices."

"Dolly's fifteen and so is Easton."

"It wasn't sex, and we all knew the risks. If you had any idea how hard we worked—"

"I could lose my job and you kids could be out of school."

James lit a cigarette. Jeremy resisted the urge to ask for one. *They knew the risks.* He exhaled the smoke straight up into the air. The wind blew waves, like scales, on the lake. The snowflakes were red embers falling from the sky. It was like a bomb went off—somewhere so close that Jeremy braced for the aftershock.

"I'll take the fall," James said.

Jeremy babbled about how they were all falling and that none of them would be at Nat Mota after this. He imagined Orleans at fifteen. "Why didn't you think? Why didn't I think? Who the hell are you trying to get back at, James?"

When James didn't say anything, Jeremy imagined Dolly crying in her room as she prepared to run away. He imagined Donald writing a formal statement, putting distance between the school and the foolish teacher. He thought Donald would call it a treaty between him and the newspapers. Jeremy thought that tomorrow all of the criminals would be in the newspapers, damned along with pornographers and rapists, gunmen and drug dealers—all the terrorists. "You didn't have to include me."

"I thought you'd be proud of us."

Jeremy expected someone to say *Cut!*, that the red snow would suddenly stop falling, that they would go back to their dressing rooms and try to get a better take the next day.

"Will you at least watch the movie with me?" James said, his voice quiet enough to melt snowflakes. "So I can explain."

And then there they were, James and Jeremy, sitting in front of the television. Darla had Orleans in the bath, washing her with some of the cockroach soap. Orleans screamed/sang, *Mama's getting the sea painted green, so I'm washin', washin' washin' in the wild wild West,* and Jeremy dog-eared the sound of her voice, saving it for a saner moment. James narrated his director moves—the why, the how, the where. He pressed pause when he wanted to make something clear. *See this? See that?* he said, and Jeremy wondered what the point of this screening exercise was. The film finished, and just as James said, "You taught me how to write that," a bare-naked Orleans ran into the living room and planted a big kiss on Jeremy's lips. She looked at James. "Goodnight, Dad's stu-dent!" She ran to her bedroom, her rear end shiny and damp.

James looked after her and smiled, embarrassed. He looked away when he saw Jeremy watching him. The roof contracted from the cold. The sky that had been ulcerous was now black. Jeremy stared at the ceiling, inhaled, and exhaled from fully inflated cheeks. James scooted forward on the couch and turned to him. "I'm sorry about any trouble I've caused for Dolly and Easton." James tried to look at the snow falling outside the window but only saw Jeremy's and his reflection. Something changed in James' face; he became more confident. "It's a protest," he said. "The body. We're fighting for it, instead of against it."

"A protest?" Jeremy said.

—

Later, a candle on the dresser made Darla's freckles dance. Jeremy kissed her, placed his hand on her abdomen. The lines in her skin guided him, the Braille of the child they created. She laid her arm across his chest and he drifted into a heavy, dream-filled sleep where he was up on the roof, spraying water onto the snow-covered trees. Soon icicles formed. He wanted to stay in the dream, watching the tragic beauty of winter, but something tugged at him, pulling him into consciousness. He opened his eyes and believed he was still dreaming, but then he smelled the burning candle. Orleans, her hair messy with sleep, stood on a chair next to his dresser where the candle sputtered. She was so little. She stared into the light and reached toward the candle. He raised his hand, as if he could stop her from the bed. He tried to speak but was unable. Something inside of him said, *You are not dreaming this movie, this movie is not your dream.* Orleans dipped a finger into the candle, the hollow formed by the flame. He felt a moment of terror from which he gathered the strength to pull the cord from the dream projector and tear his head from the cavity of sleep. She pulled her finger back, quickly, just as he managed to say, "Orleans." He leaned out of the bed, almost falling on his face.

"Dad?" Her finger was red with candle wax.

"Orleans," Jeremy said, louder than he meant to.

"Nighttime voice," she commanded. "Mom's sleeping." He sighed, and she looked at her waxed digit. "Dad, look, it's stuck to my finger. It didn't even burn." She walked toward the bed, her finger extended. By the time she took the few steps, Jeremy was on his knees. He grabbed her around the waist and squeezed her. She wrapped her skinny arms around his head and face. The soft wax covering the tip of her finger brushed against his whiskers. "You're squeezing too hard, Dad. Don't you want to see?"

"Sorry. I'm sorry, Orleans. You scared me is all." Jeremy pulled her into bed and she was asleep as soon as her head hit his chest. He moved her so that she was also against her mother. When he placed his hand on Darla's arm, they were all touching. As he fell into the fog of pre-sleep, he imagined that he heard snow falling on the roof. He waited, his eyes open, hoping snow would cover the city, the streets, the house, and that in the morning everything would be frozen solid and the three of them, together, would be forever trapped inside their home.

WOE TO YOU, DESTROYER (WHO YOURSELF HAVE NOT BEEN DESTROYED)

for Rabbit and Sissy

HUMPING A GREASE-SPATTERED BACKPACK, GI entered the east side of Cheesman Park. Two men, his friends, followed, and Nellie, pushing a shopping cart, brought up the rear. A morning breeze washed over the park and they walked to the Grecian pavilion that had once offered a panorama of Denver, a view now blocked by cottonwoods and condos. A century before, the park had been a cemetery, and some said that Cheesman was haunted by the ghosts of those who had been dug up and deposited elsewhere. Like these ghosts, GI was disconnected from his past, most of which was forgotten. He was a shadow lost from the object that had intercepted the light in the first place.

A hundred-year heat wave bore down on Denver. The pavilion was surrounded by dried rose bushes with chapped and puckered blossoms, dead grass, and yellowed cottonwoods. The ground ached for water. "Let's stop and have a nip," GI said. Chico and Ted set their backpacks on the pavilion floor and leaned against them. GI pulled out the remains of last night's bottle, and Nellie sat down, her back to him.

"I don't want to stay no more where we did last night," Nellie said.

"No one asked you to go in there with him," Chico said.

"Nellie," Ted said, "Martyred Mother of Our Cause."

"I'll tell you two to shut it just once," GI said. He handed the bottle to Nellie. Yesterday, after Ted had scored a fifty-dollar bill by holding a sign, they had visited Julius's apartment, smoked grass, and slept in his air-conditioned living room. Nellie had bartered with Julius, and Ted still had most of the fifty.

117

In the pavilion, Nellie now sang, "Happy birthday to you, happy birthday dear Tommy."

Chico rolled a thin cigarette. He said, "This is the fourth birthday that kid's had in about as many weeks."

"Shut it," GI said.

"It's no use encouraging her delusions," Chico said.

Nellie stood and looked down on Chico. "You're the only delusion I see," she said. She closed and opened her eyes, and then snarled at Chico for refusing to disappear. They watched as Nellie pushed her cart off the pavilion and across the road that snaked through the park and onto the rolling lawn below. She pulled a blanket from the cart, spread it on the grass, and removed her jacket. The men continued to drink from the bottle but found it hard to remove their gaze from Nellie. "You're finding out like I did," Chico said. "The hard way."

"She only did it for us. Don't try to bring her down." GI's voice was deep and scratched. He rolled a cigarette. The rising sun infected the sky with the oranges and yellows of cancer. "I shouldn't of let her do it."

"That's what I'm getting at, bro," Chico said. "You think you got a hold on what she does." GI handed Chico the rolling papers and the tobacco. "She does what she wants, and you can't be thinking she's doing something *for* you. That ain't the way that gal works. And I—"

"Should know," GI said. "How many times *you* told me that?"

"Relax, fellas," Ted said. "You're ruining the only pleasant time of day." He pulled on his smoke-stained gray moustache. "Now look at that sweet lady." Nellie's shirt was rolled to the base of her breasts, sun shining on her belly and legs, both browned like cigar paper. "Dear Martyred Mother," Ted said.

GI tossed his cigarette. Smoke slowly vented from his mouth and nose, lingering about his head as if his insides smoldered. He burned for Nellie. Her refusal to honestly love him back sparked his shame. She had little regard for herself and certainly none for him. She did what she wanted—she was prideful and vain—*and* she stayed by his side. A study in contradiction. GI wondered if he loved her more because she loved him less, loved him with an inconsistency that gave him headaches.

Last night, she had traded herself so that they might sleep safely. There was the heat, yes, but more threatening were the murders—serial murders committed against Denver's homeless. GI, Nellie, Chico, and Ted had been sleeping together under the Federal Bridge—GI believed in the safety of numbers. They didn't need to stay at Julius's, and yet he did nothing to stop Nellie. This wasn't the first time he had seen Nellie barter. When they first met, she named a price, and he had paid. There were others, too. Always others.

Julius's apartment was a dim cave, boxes and bulging green garbage bags littering the floor. "I lost my job at the hospital, so it's time to get my git on," he had said. "I'm moving 'cross town, down near the 'Fax and Five Points, the po-po station." Julius spat on his floor.

GI knew Julius from when he had worked at the Nat Mota school as a handyman, this from way back in the mid-1980s. Julius had been a smartass, know-it-all student. GI sold some LSD to Julius, and the wrong people heard about it. GI had been fired and then took a shit job at the Purina factory. Fifteen years since that quarter-bag, and here they were, both skidded off the tracks.

"You staying safe out there?" Julius said. GI said that tempers were as high as the heat. The shelters were overrun, but GI didn't mention that Nellie refused to stand in line at them. "Everyone's afraid of waking up dead," he said. Julius had laughed, his mouth open, revealing two rows of silver-capped molars that flashed like miniature chainsaw blades. "I wake up dead nearly every day," Julius said. "That's what gives me my pleasant disposition."

Around midnight, when they made to leave, Julius winked at Nellie and said that they could sleep on the floor. GI hefted his bag. Nellie said, "Might as well." Julius swiped his tongue across his front teeth. GI set his bag on the floor, the air conditioning hissing a wicked coldness, and Nellie followed Julius to his bedroom. They unrolled their sleeping bags and listened as the bedsprings in the other room creaked a broken rhythm. Julius grunted and GI lit a cigarette. He pictured himself sticking a knife in Julius, slicing him like the pig he was. Finally, the springs stopped. GI closed his eyes but knew Nellie was next to him. He opened his eyes and he and Nellie looked like nothing more than shadows existing in a single dimension—no depth, no time. She smelled sour and salty. She touched him and the dimensions returned. Her skin was damp, and when she spoke he was surprised that she was not out of breath. Did she even live in her own body? She whispered, "I want my boy back."

Nellie's boy, Tommy, lived with a foster family in South Dakota or maybe Georgia. At the Fort Golan hospital they had given Nellie the juice so many times that her memories leaked right through, spilling behind her. Chico didn't believe that Tommy existed at all. GI himself had two kids whose faces he had not seen in over ten years. Even if he could conjure them, by now he wouldn't have recognized them on the street. He believed Nellie. He knew Nellie's pain, the anguish of lack, and he wanted to give her something more. He wanted to get up enough money to go to Key West, where he pictured Nellie sunbathing—she was the only homeless woman he had ever seen sunbathe—and they would spare-change the tourists and sleep on the beach. No heat waves, no murders, no homeless kids who prowled the streets like rabid dogs.

Nellie looked innocent in the sun. When she went to Julius, he could have said, *No*. At Julius's, she had reached into GI's sleeping bag and pulled out his hand, kissed it, held it to her damp cheek. GI watched her and prayed:

Lord, be gracious to us. Thank you, Lord, for these drops of whiskey we share. Thank you for letting us wake alive. Keep us safe from the things that want to destroy us. He quietly prayed her name. *Nellie.* He said her name until he was dreaming Key West and they swam in the ocean and kissed salty kisses. *Nellie.*

In front of Denver Drug & Liquor, they waited for Ted. Nellie insisted on crossing the street, and GI tried to get her to wait. A zit-faced kid with a BMX bike and Chico exchanged words, and GI reached for Nellie as she stepped from the curb. Suddenly, the kid lifted the BMX and slammed it into Chico's upper body and just as quickly the kid was on the bike, across the street, and down the block before the first drop of blood hit the sidewalk. In the confusion, Ted and Nellie headed toward the river, and GI tended to Chico, who was dazed but still standing. GI looked around, waiting for the kid to return, but it was the cops that smelled the blood.

He sat in the back of the squad car, a free ride to detox, which for the officers meant less paperwork than a public drunkenness ticket. He knew the squad car well, number 723, belonging to Officer Victor Codaz, whom GI and the boys less than affectionately referred to as the Dick of District Six. But Codaz was riding shotgun and a face that he did not recognize stared back at him in the mirror.

"You don't recognize me, do you, Lawrence?"

GI laughed and said, "I'm not likely sober when I'm picked up by the likes of you."

The cop driving the car slammed on the brakes and quickly accelerated, throwing GI forward and then back, his weight slamming his cuffed wrists into the fiberglass seat.

"You ever wonder what it's going to be like to burn in hell?" Codaz said.

"I don't need your Jesus lectures," GI said.

"You could use an eternity's worth of Jesus lectures."

"I know the story. He suffered to get you off scot-free. I don't need no one to suffer publicly for me. I suffer publicly near every day."

The squad car passed the entryway to the detox center, which looked like a fortified emergency room entrance. As they continued to drive, GI thought he was instead headed to jail. He studied the cop's face, feeling like he knew the man. He felt a terrible dread. They drove down Thirteenth, west, turned south and then west again on Highway 6, out of Denver County and into Jefferson County, pulling off at the fairgrounds exit. GI remained silent. They stopped in a secluded pull-off.

The cops got out of the car and opened the back door behind which GI sat silent, hands still cuffed behind his back. Victor grabbed GI's arm and spun him around, against the car. "Your suffering, Stuart, is not the suffering of Christ. It's neglect." Pressing his elbow against GI's cheek, Victor stuck his hand into GI's pocket, pulled out two singles, a few quarters and nickels. These Victor put in his own pocket.

"Let me re-introduce you to Officer Charlie Ravenna," Codaz said.

GI stood unbelieving—Charlie Ravenna, his former brother-in-law. Since when had he been a cop here in Denver? GI seemed to remember that he was a sherriff in some backwater in Arkansas.

"I wish I could say it's a pleasure to see you again," Charlie said.

"I'm not proud of what I done," GI said. "I've asked for Janice's forgiveness."

"You haven't seen those kids in a decade, not that they would want to see you or what you've become."

Charlie paused and GI searched his face and found a deep and residing kindness there. This was a good man in front of him, but GI knew that Charlie wanted nothing more than to cause him personal harm.

"I'm new to town, but last week, my second day on the force, I found a man dead, leg sawed right off," Charlie said. "His face was in the dirt and knowing you was tramping here in Denver, I was hoping to flip the body and see your face."

"I suppose that's natural," GI said. Charlie yanked on GI's hands, which remained cuffed. GI stood on his tiptoes, but the pain screamed through his wrists and shoulders. In a single motion, Charlie released the cuffs and GI's hands went slack against his sides. Charlie spun him around and slapped his open hand into GI's chest. GI kept his eyes on Charlie, but he sensed that something had fallen to the ground.

"The eight-mile walk will do you good," Codaz said. "Must be over a hundred today."

GI stood with his arms at his sides, and only when the car faded into the distance did he reach down and pick up the photograph of a girl and a boy, maybe ten and eight years old, sitting on a beach beside a sand castle. They had such genuine looks of happiness on their faces that he wanted to sink to the ground and dream himself back to a time when he might have done something that would make a bit of difference. Ginny and Bobby. These were his children, and he could not for the life of him decide whether Charlie in giving him the photo had done him some great charity or an even greater injustice.

He began to walk. He was no stranger to walking. It would be dark by the time he got back. Nellie and Ted would have settled in somewhere. They had been moving about a lot recently, and some nights Ted and Chico opted to stay in the shelters, but not Nellie. Not him either. GI began moving his legs forward, step after step. Eight miles of steps before he reached Denver, more before he found Nellie.

Nellie slept under the bridge, slept like a dead person. Chico and Ted had left to get lunch at the shelter. GI was hungry, but Nellie made fun of the folks standing in the lines—food lines, bed lines, water lines—and now GI was too embarrassed to wait for anything.

Two days before, Jimmy Aces was found dead. Jimmy was a former blackjack dealer in Vegas who was fond of showing off his tricks, and in death his cards had been spread around him, a bloody queen of hearts attached to his forehead. The day before, a homeless woman had been raped before she was killed. The cops found a dead black kid that morning. Rumors and theories were exchanged—turf wars between the old boys and the young dicks, the Freight Train Riders of America, the cops. Nellie had no theories about the murders. "Who hasn't been destroyed before?" she said. GI now carried a screwdriver in his pocket. Recently, he had traded some of his tools—tape measure, level, and chisel—for a Bowie knife.

Nellie was awake now, rubbing sleep from her eyes. "You need to take a sign to the street," she said. He said that he didn't want to leave her alone. Under her breath, she mocked him, and his face went flush. "I don't need anybody to look after me." Nellie stood at her cart sorting clothing, looking at scraps of paper.

"If you don't need nobody to look after you, why do you need *me* to hold a sign?"

A helicopter circled overhead and Nellie swatted at it. "Fucksake." She stood up and lifted her arms to the sky. "If you going to follow me all the time, you might as well make some use of yourself." She picked through her shopping cart, lifting blankets, clothes, undergarments. A boom box.

"Why not come with me?" GI said.

"Quit with your look, like you don't know if you want to fuck me or set me on your knee. And quit talking to every man like you *own* me or know what's best for me."

GI pulled a cardboard sign from his pack. Years ago, he told people that he was the first to put *veteran* on his signs, and they had called him GI ever since. He never said Vietnam, but people assumed just the same. He had the photograph of his children in his army jacket pocket. He had mulled over showing the photograph to Nellie but he could not risk her ridicule, not on this.

"I was out here long before I met you, making my way in good times and bad." She claimed to receive disability checks, but he never saw her go to a post-office box. Nellie squatted in

SO MANY TRUE BELIEVERS

the bushes, her shorts and panties around her ankles. How many other men had stood before her while she pissed? She lacked modesty. She was vain. He wished he had the will to turn his head. Hiking up her shorts, Nellie stuck out her tongue. "I'd be happy, GI, if you would just go hold the sign for a party tonight." She cupped his chin in her hand. "Don't look so upset."

"What if we left, Nellie? Me and you." She stepped back, her eyes fearful. She had once told him that the electroconvulsion therapy stopped her from committing suicide. "Key West, Florida, Nellie. That's what I'm thinking."

"You can't even get us money for a bottle. How you going to get us to Florida?"

"You're wrong, Nellie. I can get us there." Ducks floated north on the Platte, and it occurred to GI that that was the wrong direction for a river to flow.

Nellie laughed. "Look at the rooster," she said. She pointed to GI and turned her head to look at the ducks floating by. "He's got his gander up, he does." She laughed, but the corners of her mouth were down again. "I'll go if you get us there," she said.

GI returned from holding the sign and Nellie's cart remained hidden behind a scrubby bush, his backpack wedged in beside it. She was nowhere to be seen. He held two bottles of beer, two cheeseburgers, a bag of fries, and a Baby Ruth bar, Nellie's favorite. Holding the sign had been hot work, the standing, the asphalt, the cars and buses. GI's skin felt like one giant blister ready to burst. He wanted to drink down one of the beers, or better, both beers, but he waited for Nellie. He pulled his sleeping bag from his pack and pushed it up against the bridge wall. She'd be back in a minute and they'd have a little party, fight off the heat with a summer celebration. As he fell asleep, he imagined the smile she would give him when she saw the Baby Ruth bar.

As he often did after holding the sign, he dreamed of two small, faceless children looking out the back window of a station wagon, waving, sticking out their tongues. In the dreamscape, after seeing the children, he would feel fear and then confusion. But this time, they had faces—the faces from the photograph—and he startled awake, sweating in shame and anger.

A dry wind blew over the riverbed and paper rattled. He looked toward the sound, thinking schools and notebooks, and saw Nellie's shopping cart, the bottom lined with newspaper. "Nellie?" he said. No answer. He waited and listened. Their rules had been clear about keeping track of each other at night. "Nellie!" His voice cracked. She wasn't near. He heard someone laugh just upstream. "Hey," GI said. "You see anyone by the name of Nellie?"

"Don't know anyone named Nellie, so I might and I might not," was the answer that came back. GI rolled up his sleeping bag. Fishing through his pack, he pulled out the two beers and stuffed the sleeping bag inside the pack. He drank from one of the beers and tried to think, but he only saw the front-page newspaper pictures—bodies bagged and caught in a web of police tape. "Nellie!"

GI took a notebook and pen from the pack then taped the note to a tree. He threw the pack on the shopping cart and headed down the hill.

Chico stood on South Santa Fe Drive holding a sign and just below him GI and Ted sat alongside the Platte River in the shade, smoking and watching the river slowly move north. "I think you ask him," Ted said. "Sometimes those we least expect will show kindness." GI grunted. He leaned on Nellie's cart. He threw a pebble into the water and watched it vanish. "It wouldn't hurt is all I'm saying," Ted said.

"It *would* hurt," GI said. Traffic flowed from both Santa Fe and the Valley Highway, I-25. GI had been searching for Nellie almost nonstop for a week now. Chico said that hanging signs was a waste of time, but Ted said that signs worked for missing dogs and cats; why shouldn't they for a missing woman? GI had checked with the police and at Fort Golan, but these were both a dead end. He didn't know Nellie's last name. Searching through the cart had turned up nothing. He wondered if her name was really Nellie. There was no ID in the cart and no check stubs. Without any identification, she couldn't cash any checks. He hadn't let the cart out of his sight, not since she disappeared. Even at night, his hand touched its wheel. When he found her, she would thank him for keeping such good care of all her things, all her possessions—her pictures of Tommy, her lady things, her winter clothes, her magazines.

GI stood at Nellie's cart. He felt guilty picking through her things like he had, but it had been necessary. Now he peeled the blanket back and folded it. A black bikini sat on top and he ran his hand over the shiny fabric.

GI pushed Nellie's cart and for a moment the rattle of its stainless steel and rubber wheels was inaudible. Construction surrounded them—cranes, bulldozers, jackhammers—the sounds of progress. The old Forney Transportation Museum was wrapped in chain-link. They were building a new sporting goods store, a flagship. GI remembered how when his kids were small he and Janice had taken them to the Forney. GI guessed that the building was almost 100,000 square feet. Their tour guide had been a bearded man with a gimp arm, and as they moved through the museum, stuffed full of antique cars, planes, and trains, Janice had said she was creeped-out. Cobwebs hung over everything, and manikins were crudely clothed in the period of the vehicles they surrounded. The cars did not shine, the motorcycles did not seem fast—the entire museum was like a haunted house and they had joked that the museum would make an excellent location for a Dirty Harry chase scene.

Now, walking away from the building, GI felt like he belonged inside it, back in the past among the dusty and ill-positioned manikins, the rusted engines and tattered upholstery. No one cared about that past. They hadn't cared when it was in disrepair, and they didn't care now that it would only be a memory. GI felt like a relic, one without value.

The boys kept walking, the skyscrapers of downtown off to their left. They approached Colfax. GI saw Charlie and Codaz parked in a lot next to Colfax and Speer. They were eating sandwiches and appeared to be watching the traffic. Charlie smiled when the three men approached. He stepped from his vehicle and placed his cap on his head.

"I need your help, Charlie. I wouldn't be asking if I wasn't desperate." Charlie looked equal parts entertained and bored. "I wouldn't ask you for a thing. Not ever. I know you don't like me." GI listened to the traffic grunt and halt, sigh and start. A helicopter flew overhead, moving slowly across the sky, as if a model in the hands of some child who at any moment would play havoc on this toy city of buildings, dirt, and plastic people. "It's Nellie. She's been gone for weeks."

"That's his woman," Officer Codaz said. "She's a Colfax prost."

"I don't know her last name." GI's voice cracked. "I've searched everywhere and talked to just about everyone I thought could help."

Codaz laughed and walked away. Charlie nodded and rubbed his jaw. He looked beyond the men and into the dense city landscape rising beyond Speer. "I haven't spoken with her."

"But you've seen her?" GI's voice sounded like a child's, filled with want. "Would you tell me where, Charlie?"

"It's only speculation, Lawrence. I don't want to get your hopes up. What you really need to do is file an MPR."

"I've tried, but I don't know her last name," GI whispered.

"I heard she got picked up and taken to Golan," Charlie said.

GI exhaled. He dug a cigarette from his pocket, lit it. The clouds moved from his vision, receding to the edges of his sight.

"I think I saw her with Julius Sisto," Codaz said from the front seat of the cruiser.

"I thought she might be dead," GI said.

"I've talked to Julius," Chico said, "and he don't know where she is."

"Like I said, I *think* I saw her with Sisto. Once or twice on Colfax. Late one night, Sisto helped her get into a car. My guess is he's pimping her."

"I talked to him two days ago," Chico said. "He hadn't seen her."

The radio barked from his squad car. "If you'll excuse me," Charlie said." He walked to the car, stopped, and turned around. "We took her to Golan, Lawrence. If she's dead, we'll be sure to find you."

GI braced himself against the shopping cart. GI couldn't blame Charlie, not after the way he had treated Janice and the kids. He had a memory that rose like vapor from a manhole cover—the girl wetting her pants...him locking her outside one winter night...by daylight, the social workers descending on the house, escorting the children away... He threw a blanket on the memory, disappearing the ghost but not the humiliation.

Nellie could still be at Fort Golan, but then again, the people at Golan said that it didn't matter what her last name was—they had no woman of Nellie's description there. If she had left, she could be anywhere, somewhere out in Denver looking for GI. *She was alive.* Nellie, her sweet body. Nellie, her stern voice. Nellie was out there. GI was convinced. He looked beyond the steep banks of the Platte, the beautiful, stupid, backward river, and he smiled for the first time since she had gone missing.

On an embankment just behind the Six Flags amusement park, GI had Nellie's and his possessions spread out on the concrete. He scratched his head and did some quick math and while some things he immediately knew the price of, others he needed to guesstimate. Charcoal $5—it said so right on the bag. He scratched down $14.00 for the small barbeque grill. The tools were worth more than anything, with the exception of Nellie's lady stuff. $75.00. The two backpacks, ten apiece; black markers, $6.00. Cooler, $15.00. Two twenty-four-ounce beers inside the cooler, $2.35. And how to price Nellie's lady stuff?—bras and underwear of different sizes and materials, wigs, dresses, a couple of bathing suits, and makeup in tubes, canisters, and compacts. GI's head spun. $200 was the best he could guess. And then there was other shit, random clothing, shoes, things, and more things. $100, maybe. All totaled it was nearly $400.

People ran stalls at the Mile High Flea Mart, but they gave bottom dollar on everything. He could pawn the tools. Nellie would be pissed if he sold her things, but he wasn't even sure where Nellie was, *if* she was, but, if she was, and he found her, they could get the hell out of Denver, maybe could rent a place, and he could work where they wouldn't garnish child support. GI and Nellie would go to Key West, Florida, or New Orleans, Louisiana, anywhere but Denver, Colorado.

Although it was over one hundred degrees, Julius wore a two-piece suit—a stained, white tank top under the jacket. He was working the streets early today. Julius scratched at the black growth on his face and nodded. "I don't know if I can help." Julius looked to the sky, kicked at a cigarette butt sitting near his tennis shoe. He offered GI a cigarette, and GI quickly took it. Julius smiled. "You know in my line a work, I can't just go telling a John where a girl is—even if she ain't mine. People have ulterior motives."

GI lifted the shopping cart and slammed it down. "She ain't no whore."

With a toothpick, Julius dug at his nails. "Where you been?"

"I'm telling you." GI shook his dirty finger at Julius. Julius laughed. "I'll fucking break you," GI said. He poked Julius's chest. Julius grabbed the finger and twisted it hard, the knuckles popping and folding. "Sonofabitch," GI said through gritted teeth. Julius twisted again. A sound came from Julius's mouth, a guttural pig's squeal. GI cried out in pain and fell to the ground. His forehead rolled against the pavement and he inched himself toward the shopping cart. Looking up, he saw Julius's dirty tennis shoes, the creased pant legs, and the smiling face and silver-capped teeth. "Stupid, stupid, stupid," Julius said. He placed his shoe on GI's shoulder and gently rolled back and forth. GI crawled toward the shopping cart; he reached for it with his left hand. Julius's foot came down on GI's arm, and pushing his full weight forward, Julius reached into his back pocket. "You are one sorry piece of shit, always have been. Everything you touch turns to shit, but I guess it's because you are shit." GI stood, cradled the broken finger, and stepped toward Julius. "Quit while you're ahead," Julius said. He opened his jacket, a sheathed knife tucked inside his waistband.

"But when you run into Nellie." Julius unzipped his red trousers and pulled out his cock. GI looked away. "Hey, garbage man, when you run into Nellie, you let her know she can get her stuff back. All she's got to do is wrap her lips around this." Julius tucked himself back in his pants. "I bet you never even seen her dressed in any of this, GI." Julius held up a black bra and underwear. He dug through the clothes with one hand and pushed the cart with the other. He walked north toward Speer, the cart sounding a steady metal rattle. "See ya around. Here." Julius tossed a roll of duct tape at GI. "Fix that fucking finger; looks like you had it up your ass."

GI bent down and picked up the tape. A pigeon approached, its neck a series of hinges, opening and closing, its eyes two small, green jewels waiting to be plucked.

GI felt broken and naked. The pain was lessened by a few hits off a bottle some generous soul had offered him. Initially, his finger looked like a short snake in an s-pattern, but as it swelled it looked more like an overboiled hot dog, meat zigzagged as it broke from the skin. He bought two flasks of whiskey, which he stuffed into his pants and covered with his shirt. The idea was to drink alone. When he began the descent to the bridge at Colfax over the Platte, he saw her. She was muttering to herself, but she looked sober and well-fed. She laughed when she saw him, but then as he continued climbing down, she began to frantically look around the area underneath the bridge. She scanned the concrete underside, the grass on the embankments, and even the bridge rafters. When GI was ten feet away, he said her name. *Nellie.*

"GI."

"Some people thought you might be dead."

"I ain't."

"I see that." Pigeon shit fell from the rafters. They both raised their eyes to the birds and the mound of white and black shit piling on the sill. "I didn't like that you were gone without any word. We need to look out for each other, Nellie."

"Did you look after my stuff?"

GI pulled a bottle from his pants. "I did, Nellie. I had your cart with me the whole time." He paused, tried to decide: truth or lie. "I had it all the whole time. I swear."

"Fucking cops. There was no reason for it. Where's my cart?"

"Julius."

"Why in hell would Julius have my shit?"

"Look at my finger." GI held it up in the air. The finger looked as crooked as the letters he drew in the love message he had left for her.

"Fuck your finger!" Nellie stood and pushed GI in the shoulder. "He's got it all?"

"Nellie, I'll get the stuff back. I've got a plan for us, a plan for somewhere else." GI held his hand away from Nellie, and they both sat down on a piece of cardboard. GI searched the darkened underbelly of the bridge for something he recognized, some material thing he could pull to him but there was only Nellie, who would refuse him if he tried to touch her. Two mallards floated by. A male and a female both interbred with other ducks, misfits. Amid piles of brown foam, the ducks floated into the reeds, dipped their heads into the polluted water, and drank. The bird's bellies were stained from the Platte and Cherry Creek rivers. The birds never left Denver. Even in the winter, they could feast on the grass at the always-green golf courses, but they lived short lives as they absorbed the poisons that industry dumped into the rivers. They didn't know any better—a poisonous life was the only one they had ever known.

"Julius do that to your finger?" Nellie lightly poked at the crippled digit. GI flinched and awaited her touch again. She ran her fingers along GI's, from the fingernail, following the s-curve down to the base, touched his thumb, and held his wrist. "It hurts worse than bad, Nell. I swear to Christ, I'll get everything back together for us. Everything and then we'll get the fuck out of here." Nellie pulled GI to her breast, and she rubbed his head. GI wet her shirt, saliva and tears, wet kisses. "I thought you were dead, Nell. I don't care about my finger."

The hammer was heavy in GI's pocket. He had followed Julius for two late afternoons and early evenings—out of his apartment, down to the diner, and back to where he'd pick up more weed. Julius had once taught GI to pick locks, and now GI entered Julius's locked apartment. He wanted a cigarette. There was a pack on the table. In the corner, next to a barstool and a stack of empty beer cans, sat a garbage bag, a black bra hanging out of the bag like the intestine of a punctured stomach. GI walked over to the bag, opened it, and breathed in the smell of Nellie's lady things, of everything that Nellie owned. He closed the bag and winced in pain. Nellie had used the duct tape to secure his index finger to his middle finger.

All he had to do was heft the bag over his shoulder and walk out the door. He had seen Nellie's cart in the alley. Leaving quickly had been the idea. When it came down to it, he was no match for Julius. Julius was younger, stronger, and meaner.

When GI heard footsteps on the porch, he hid behind the door and slipped the claw hammer from his pocket. The door opened and GI swung the hammer as hard as his bad finger would allow. There was a loud crack, two low grunts—one from each of the men, and Julius fell to the ground. GI dropped the hammer and it brushed his leg as it fell, leaving behind a wisp of blood and small pieces of tooth. He leaned down and pulled Julius's money clip from his pants, took every bill inside, and then threw the wallet back on Julius's face. "Show you," he said. He grabbed the hammer and the garbage bag and was out the door.

GI would take the cart down to Nellie, convince her to move, and then head to the Greyhound station. She was down under the bridge at Colfax and Speer. All told it would take them an hour, maybe less.

When GI opened the door, he saw Charlie sitting in car 723. The bag was in GI's good hand, the hammer dangling from the broken one. He dropped the bag and switched the hammer to his other hand. Charlie stepped from the car and said, "Police. Get your hands where I can see them."

GI looked from side to side to see where Codaz might be. Where there was one cop, there were more cops. Codaz approached from the right, gun held high. GI lifted the hammer and decided that he would destroy every goddamned unkind thing. Charlie stepped toward GI, his gun now drawn. GI imagined Nellie under the bridge and calling his name as he had called hers when she was missing. He imagined her calling the three names he was given at birth—*Lawrence Saul Stuart*. He could see her standing on the bank of the creek with her hands to her mouth and he swore that a sound, a sound that was like her voice hissing his name in prayer, dropped from the sky and landed in his ears, blanketing everything in darkness.

THE MERMAID

MADELYN PHONES ME BECAUSE OUR TWO CHILDREN are hounding her with requests to spend winter break with friends, whose respective families will vacation in Paris and maybe San Diego. I'm not positive of the destinations—Madelyn knows—but the point is they want to go somewhere without us. To the best of my knowledge, we were not planning to go anywhere.

"Maybe we should plan something, Harold," Madelyn says. "It's been a long time since we've vacationed. It would be like old times. And maybe good for all of us."

"Yes. Old times." I work for Land O' Chow in pet food development, and I now glance at the product performance reviews on my desk, information quantifiable and thus understandable.

"We could go back to St. Augustine," she says.

"Are you sure about this?" I tell Madelyn that I will make the reservations, knowing that Courtney and James will be disappointed. Madelyn and I used to go to St. Augustine every year. It's where we met, and the beaches hold some dear memories for two people who no longer say *Do you remember when?* and instead dwell upon *How can I forget that you did that?* The past few years our family vacations were forgettable experiences: I worked, Madelyn shopped, the kids brought friends or they didn't bring friends, and everyone engaged in a separate agenda. The urgency with which Madelyn insists on a *family* vacation foretells of a drastic increase in shared-time requirements. There will be specific and lengthy family outings, maybe guided tours, or even bicycle rentals. All seem painful.

I often wish I were given to hobbies, perhaps a man who goes home and loses himself building a ship inside a bottle. But I'm not that man. I stay late at the office, sometimes staring at the single picture-lined wall. In the middle is a photograph of Madelyn and me standing on opposite sides of Father Winston, repeating our vows. There are several shots of us looking tanned and fit beneath the St. Augustine sun. Surrounding these are photographs of the children—birthdays, holidays, First Communions, and such. As the pictures fan out from the center, we all get a little older, and our smiles and embraces are replaced with posed stoicism and peculiar distances. I have not added to the collage in two years.

"Are you finding a place in your heart for forgiveness, Harold?" Father Winston says. Madelyn and I sit in the Father's office for our biweekly marriage counseling session. Our chairs are arranged in a circle—perhaps a triangle—so we might convene as equals to discuss our faith and our wandering from the path of righteousness. Time stutters by during these sessions as I worm around uncomfortably and my chair moves farther and farther from the circle's center.

"I am trying to bring my family love in the way that I know how," I say. "I provide. I am waiting for the seas of my hardened heart to part, then I will walk between the waves and into—"

"That's very poetic, Harold," Father Winston says, "but are you willing to forgive?"

Madelyn looks at Father Winston and then at me, searching and waiting. She grips the padded leather arms of her chair and takes a deep breath, holding it for two seconds, and then she slowly deflates.

"I've acknowledged my mistake and made myself a better person," Madelyn says. "I don't know what else to do."

Madelyn's infidelity stripped me of everything I invested in our marriage. Another man inside her thrust me from my role as lover, husband, and father. Madelyn belonged to me—she was a virgin when we met. Our children know of Madelyn's infidelity, and thus I haven't done the best job of restraining the flood of hurt. I am left less of a man, less of a father.

"It's really a matter of looking within yourself, Harold," Father Winston says. "Too often people concentrate on trying to blame, when healing is found not by casting stones but by changing your own perspective. Shine your stones, if you will. Focus on what you love, not on what you find distasteful."

I met Madelyn at a church retreat in St. Augustine, Florida, and one night after Bible study, I asked her take a walk along the beach. Soon, we entered the ocean and swam out into the deeper waters. She was so young then, and her teeth were pearls that I kissed in the moonlight. I was focused on my career, but I knew I should find a wife. I expected someone to come along who would be my companion, my home-front support, but Madelyn desired night swims in the depths, champagne cocktails with breakfast, and discussions of spirituality. One year later, we married and spent our honeymoon in St. Augustine. Every year but the last three, we returned for at least a long weekend.

We were somewhat happy for the first year of our marriage, but when Courtney was born things changed. I received a promotion and became the Vice-President of Pet Food Development. More and more of my time was demanded at the office to ensure the quality, determine the palatability, and test the marketability of prototypes. People are convinced that their dogs are as worthy of a healthy life as they or their children are. Business continues to boom. Some of the younger men in the office, my employees, refer to themselves as *players* in the industry. In that case, I am a very big player in the dog food industry. They are afraid to say it, but I am not. Dog food is my life. The house, the vacations, the automobiles are luxuries we can now afford.

As my time at the office increased, Madelyn's devotion to me became less pronounced. She joined book clubs and the like that kept her away evenings. I speculated it was the course that life often runs. When she asked for a divorce two years ago, I was not shocked that she no longer wanted me to be a part of her life, but I was surprised when she said that she had reconciled the matter with God.

I came home early one day to find one of my clients, one who happens to deal in horses, wearing my bathrobe and Madelyn wearing nothing at all. My lawyer told me that although a tragic blow to my psyche, it was a fortunate discovery in that it would save me a great deal of money in the divorce proceedings. However, upon meeting with Father Winston, Madelyn quickly decided divorce was unthinkable and that she could not do it to the kids, herself, or God. Obviously she was not under contractual obligation with the initial reconciliation she made.

We have always attended Sunday services, but recently Madelyn transformed herself into a Sunday-school teacher whose simple version of faith and God's love is easily translated to children with coloring books and crayons. I doubt they color pictures of her adultery, of having the flesh from another man's back beneath her fingernails while cooking dinner for the family.

When I first met Mary Lou, I was sitting in a seventies-era diner on the avenue I go to when I'm looking for company. For reasons I cannot explain, I drank coffee in the diner each time I went to pick up a girl. I could have just driven to any number of street corners and conducted my business. Maybe the diner gave me a chance to pause and think. Anyhow, on this particular evening, a woman in a flowered polyester shirt sat by herself looking out the window and gesturing to a mongrel dog tied to a parking meter. The dog looked back at her and wagged its tail. One of her pant legs was neatly folded up and safety-pinned near the top of where a thigh should have been, and crutches leaned against the orange booth. She saw me staring at her and smiled. I had never solicited companionship until after Madelyn's request for a divorce. I went looking out of loneliness and despair. When Madelyn eventually consented to remain my wife, I had found something else, something sensual and forbidden, yet so quick and disposable. Initially, it was very easy, but the all-too-scarred presence of Mary Lou changed all of that.

I walked over to her and said, "Can I buy you a coffee?"

"I think they give free refills," she said, lifting her cup and motioning for me to sit down. Her face was reddish-tan, the brilliant pink of a sea anemone. She sipped her coffee. The heat caused her to wince, crow's feet appearing around her eyes. We were quiet for some time, and then I said, "Would you like to take a drive in my car?"

She released something like a giggle. "We could. I need to bring Dog Boy, if that's okay." She glanced at the dog sitting outside. "He doesn't bite. He's a real nice boy who looks out for his momma." She pushed herself up onto the crutches. "My name is Mary Lou, sugar."

"I'm Harold," I said. We walked outside to my car.

"Your kid's on the honor roll," she said, pointing to my bumper.

"My girl. She's a senior." The traffic moved by steadily and slowly. I felt exposed. "I can almost guarantee that she'll be at Stanford next year." Courtney is the only member of my family I have hope for. Her wish is to go to Stanford, and even though it is far from Colorado, I will not deny her. When she goes, I will be left with my wife and my son. James will go to the community college, and I imagine I will end up renting him an apartment that will get trashed and eventually raided by the police.

"My, my. Are you a Dolphins fan?" she said, smiling. She was referring to the Jesus fish Madelyn stuck on the bumper after a slight dip and then resurgence in her faith. It was a bottoming out that looks particularly alarming on a bar graph, the way the line suddenly drops and then rises higher than ever.

"No. That's my wife. I've given up... On sports."

Within fifteen minutes, we were in a parking lot a mile away. Mary Lou's head was in my lap. I put my hand into her coarse hair, and with the other I grabbed where her leg used to be. My head fell to the side, and through the Volvo's window I saw the brightly lit cross hovering above the mountains west of Denver. I did not see it as a symbol of Christ's sacrifice to mankind, but I did feel its power to judge. I turned away and looked through the sunroof at the dark clouds hiding the heavens.

While driving Mary Lou back, I couldn't help but ask her about the leg.

"It's really none of your business," she said, looking down at the dog at her foot.

"Sorry. I was just curious is all."

"Curiosity killed the cat," she said. Her eyes seemed to permanently squint.

I had wanted to know about the other girls, too, and I quickly found out that some would talk. Money talks. But I was more eager to hear this woman's story. There was the leg, or lack thereof, but there was also something about her face. It gave me the sensation of looking at the clouds and the way you can see what you want as they morph, and then as the moments pass, you find something entirely different, as if your first vision was a lie. "Would fifty dollars keep the cat alive and get him a little more informed?"

"Shit. What a sucker. Let's have the fifty bucks," she said, sticking her palm straight out, close enough to my face that I bent over and kissed it. She smelled of tobacco, of burnt offerings. "You want to hear some fish tales, baby?" And she began:

Mary Lou's Aunt Betsy took her to the carnival. Her momma was to go with them, but she was out late the night before. Behind the closed bedroom door, she coughed and then laughed something about needing more sleep. Outside, Mary Lou noticed a new dent on the car's bumper. Of all the car's dents, it was the first that was matted with hair.

Mary Lou's favorite part of the carnival cost two quarters to see. Aunt Betsy paid the barker and they stepped through a large black curtain and into the tent, the inside of which was painted with fish of many sizes and colors like they were inside an aquarium. They stepped onto a platform that overlooked a pool, straw floating on the murky water. A beautiful woman with blonde hair broke through the surface and as she swam past, the woman smiled at Mary Lou. She saw that the woman had a fish tail. "Aunt Betsy, that lady's half a fish."

Aunt Betsy, whose flowered frock was a tent itself, smiled at her. "Yes, silly. I told you before. That's a mermaid. She's half-lady, half-fish." Betsy bit into her corndog and shook her head. "No wonder Barbara's so fed up with you. You don't use your ears, girl." She held the corndog out toward Mary Lou's face. "Bite?"

Mary Lou was amazed by the fish-woman. The girl had never seen anyone so happy or so beautiful. The mermaid swam by and blew her a kiss. Mary Lou stretched to catch it. As she stepped back, her feet became entangled in thick, orange electrical cords wrapped in silver tape. Mary Lou grabbed for her aunt's fleshy hand but only came away with the corndog. She landed on her rear end and the corndog smeared her shirt with mustard.

Aunt Betsy roughly pulled her up and yanked her in the direction of the exit. "Jesus, girl. If you ain't the clumsiest thing on two legs." Mary Lou looked over her shoulder. The fish-woman grabbed the edge of the pool and pulled herself up. Mary Lou swore she heard the mermaid say, "My child. Are you okay?"

Mary Lou offered a dramatic pause. "And that's when I realized I was a mermaid. See? Just one, like a fish." She pointed to her leg. "Is that good enough?"

Mary Lou and Dog Boy got out of the car and I drove back to the highway feeling like a castaway who had found a return letter to a bottled message.

At home, when I slipped between the sheets with Madelyn, I felt as if I had entered the house through a window rather than the front door. For her part, Madelyn was a stranger wearing a green mud mask over the face that had once belonged to my wife, a face I first encountered in the waves of St. Augustine.

"It's two o'clock, Harold. You smell like a greasy breakfast."

"I worked late and stopped at a diner."

"Who works that late and stops at a diner?"

"I do."

"Yes, I forgot. You do. School called about James again."

I didn't bother to respond. I was swimming with a mermaid who swallowed salty water and playfully spit it at me.

"Thanks for your concern," she said, and moved to the far edge of the bed.

"I thought the sermon was touching," Madelyn says. We are eating a buffet brunch after church. During the sermon, Father Winston stressed the cultivation of family in these times of consumer haste. Had he written especially for us? I caught the beginning, but when I looked down the pew at my children, who heeded the sermon with the thoughtfulness of Labrador retrievers, I quit paying attention. Of course Madelyn sat with perfect posture, nodding her head in agreement.

"Yes, another winner lost on deaf ears," I say.

Madelyn holds her breath and then exhales, rolling her eyes. Under the lens of the piano music and the voices from the other tables, our silence magnifies us into strangers. I enjoy these silences.

"So how was the party, Courtney?" Madelyn says, again interrupting the soothing quiet.

"Like she's gonna tell you," James says. A piece of bacon hangs from his mouth, like a snake tongue.

"It was okay," Courtney says. Her eyes are dull and her skin unusually pale. Courtney has always been the blameless child, but now at seventeen she rounds a corner that lessens my appetite for the eggs Benedict sitting on my plate. When I woke Courtney this morning, I smelled alcohol on her sleepy breath. It wasn't the first time. I've already given up hope for James, who at fifteen only shows an interest in smoking weed and videotaping himself and his friends smoke weed. The truth is I never had much hope for him in the first place.

"Was Kurt Aldridge there? He's so cute," Madelyn says. We all stare at Madelyn. There is no masking the thoughts behind the look: *Why do you say such stupid things?* In Madelyn's defense, I am usually the recipient of these reprimanding stares, such stares that push me into silence. Madelyn, on the other hand, and to her credit, continually attempts to nurture and befriend the children.

"Yeah. He was there," Courtney says. She rises from the table and says she needs more fruit. I watch her walk away and can't help but think that she looks completely defeated.

"Roger says that he saw Kurt in the locker room one time," James says, "and he has a boa constrictor for a shlong." My wife slaps the back of his head, and I motion for the waiter to bring me more coffee.

"Won't you say something to him, Harold?" Madelyn says.

"Don't chew with your mouth open."

For a number of weeks after my first encounter with Mary Lou, I relied on luck to locate her. The past two months we have met once a week at a certain hour on a particular cross street. I draw Mary Lou a warm bath, add sea salt and then bath beads (I keep both hidden beneath an emergency kit in the trunk of the Volvo). Tonight she has her crutches and she looks well-rested. When she asks me what I would like this evening, I tell her I want nothing more than to watch her in the bath and to listen to her.

"You pay a lot of money for a lot of nonsense. Dog food must pay pretty well."

She leans out of the tub, tugging at my collar. "What is it that makes a dirty dog hungry, Harry?"

"A mermaid girl," I whisper. I lean forward to kiss her cheek,

145

and as I do, water drips off her body and pools on the floor, soaking my argyle socks.

She closes her eyes and sinks her head under the water. It is as if she is in another world, her eyes closed, her skin smoother. She rises from the shallow pool, her eyes still closed. I reach over and rub a wet, starfish nipple between my fingers. She makes dolphin sounds and opens her eyes. "Why don't you just get in here with me, Harold," she says.

"Just talk to me," I say, wishing I could hide the color rising in my cheeks. I light her a cigarette and patiently wait. I know she will give in. She has to. Everything depends on it. She flicks her ash on the floor and closes her eyes again. She speaks to me.

The television was facedown on the floor in the living room. Mary Lou knocked it over after jumping up to reach the dolphin snow globe sitting on top. Her mother screamed and sent her into the bath. Her momma's boyfriend, a beard was all Mary Lou could remember of him, found the girl and the woman in the bathroom. Momma's hands gripped Mary Lou's shoulders, holding her head under the water. He pulled her momma away. Mary Lou still lay submerged, her head submerged, when she heard the flat slap of the man's hand across her momma's face.

When her momma pulled Mary Lou out of the tub was when she started crying. She didn't remember how long she cried, but Mary Lou always assumed it was a long time if her momma felt the need to put three staples through her lips. The police and social services arrived the next day—the last day Mary Lou spent in her momma's house.

I am made a mockery of at the office. I know this. There are jokes around the water cooler about how I am a cuckold—they don't know; they just assume. My secretary listens to the belittling messages my wife leaves me about how our son's demise is my fault. On the rare occasion that I am invited to golf with the other men, they laugh at my backswing, saying it would be stronger if I took my back foot out of the grave. But it doesn't bother me because I am their boss and at the end of the day they buy drinks and joke about what bitches their wives are. All in good fun, right? They know who gives them raises.

I have written down their names alongside the things they have said to my face or behind my back. I compile this detailed list late at night when everyone has left the plant. I keep the three-ring binder locked in my desk. All of their transgressions against me are kept on record, and when I see their faces I still smile and they smile back. My wife, whose breath once smelled of another man's semen, is on the list. My son, who on one of his videotapes called me a dog-food tester, is on the list.

As I drive through the vaudeville of city lights, women in sweatshirts and jeans tight around their fleshy posteriors motion me towards them. A black man in a stocking cap whistles at me. He thinks I might want his lousy drugs. My son would; last week he was kicked out of public school for dealing pot. Now I have to send him to a private school—the Nat Mota School—that my wife found. I would have preferred a Catholic boarding school far from Denver. Fortunately though, the Nat Mota School has no admissions policies, including either skill or drug testing. The only requirement is that I write a check for sixteen-thousand dollars to cover a year's tuition. They want a lot of parental involvement. I'll leave that up to my wife—she is home all day.

I see Mary Lou spinning the wheels of her chair with gloved hands. With her deformity and her dog she belongs on this street, yet I know secrets about her that the derelicts do not. I quickly pull over to the curb and take her to a motel. It is not the thought of sex that drives me. It is something more, something that I need. I recognize the sickness, but the passion rises inside me.

When we get into the motel, I tell her to strip off her clothes. I recline next to her, touch the starfish nipples and the blowhole bellybutton, and beg her to begin.

"Come on, Harold. I'm basically a hand and blowjob girl. Parking-lot shit. This stuff is getting kind of weird." When she says my name, it's as if I've plummeted into warm water, but I refuse to tell her, knowing how she hates sentimentality and that my name will never drip from her mouth again. Although the money I place in her hands allows me to do almost anything I like, Mary Lou is in control. My being sits in her mouth, and she can chew me to bits or lick my wounds clean. Mary Lou swallows me with her second mouth and begins to move in rhythm with her speech.

After the tub incident, Aunt Betsy took her in. Betsy was kind, and she never brought men home or smelled of liquor. "My Johnny," as she referred to her dead husband, was twelve years gone. She did not need men, and the only things that entered her body besides food and air were suppositories. As she got older, Mary Lou discovered boys, or rather, she developed an understanding of boys and what they wanted. She received offers of candy for showing her white underwear. Later, a tongue kiss got her movie tickets and a backseat finger exploration was good for a couple cans of beer. It was not long before she discovered boys would give her rides in cars, buy her cigarettes, really anything she asked for, if she let them go all the way. She never fared well in school, but when she was alone with a boy, she knew it all.

Aunt Betsy noticed long before she said anything. She eventually told Mary Lou that she opened her legs as easily as her momma did. "It'll get you in trouble one of these days. You're headed down the same path as your mother, the way you use those legs of yours."

But Mary Lou did not believe Aunt Betsy. She did not use her legs like her mother because she believed her mother did not have two legs. No mother would treat her child the way Momma had. Her real mother had one leg, one beautiful leg that was a fin. She prayed every night that she would again meet the woman

148

who said, "My child. Are you okay?" Mary Lou never forgot the sound of the fish-woman's voice. Each night after her prayers the voice echoed: "My child, my child, my child." There was no doubt as to who her real mother was.

The house is in general upheaval today. We will be late for church because Courtney will not come out of her room. She says she is sick, and Madelyn informs me that the girl did not come home until four in the morning. I knock on Courtney's door, but she tells me to go away.

"This is shit," James says. "If she doesn't have to go to church, why should I?" He undoes his tie, and for a second I consider what his face might look like if I were to lift him off the ground with the tie as a noose. We go to church without Courtney and are forced to listen to James complain about the injustices of his life. He tells us all about school, how we are wasting our money, and that we should just give him the cash and he'll take his GED.

The special-education program Mary Lou attended in high school helped find her a job upon graduation. Mary Lou, however, wanted to leave Denver. She managed to get a clerical job in rural New Mexico working for a friend of her Denver employer. Living on her own was a big step. There was no Betsy at home and were no school counselors to check up on her. Although she was making do, there was still a part of her that wished she had jumped into the mermaid's pool when she had the chance.

When she filed, Mary Lou sang her ABCs (very quietly and usually just small pieces of the song). The men in the office sometimes teased her while she was singing, but she didn't mind. Monday mornings, Marty, her boss, brought donuts for everyone. Marty often stood at her desk and looked down at her. When he spoke with her, he didn't speak to her eyes but seemed to study her blouse. He often commented on her appearance, complimenting nearly everything she wore. Mary Lou let him look. She would lean in and reveal more skin. Marty would smile and she would take an extra cigarette break. Asking her in front of others to work late, Marty would occasionally take her to a hotel, giving her money afterwards, saying that he knew she wasn't paid well and that he hoped this little extra would help her get by.

Sometimes she went home with men from the bar, but not always. There was one man who made her orgasm by slowly massaging the top of her thigh. Mary Lou brought him home several times, but eventually he stopped buying her drinks. He was married, but Mary Lou was relatively sure that he stopped because she was less interested in straight sex than she was in having the thigh-inspired orgasms.

Madelyn is attending a charity event, which allows me the opportunity to go home from work and be alone. Courtney's SUV is parked outside, but I assume she rode to school with a friend. Inside, I hear someone being sick in the first-floor bathroom. I walk to the door and see my daughter perched on a stepstool with her pony-tailed head half in the toilet bowl.

"Courtney, are you okay?"

She looks up at me with a start. "I'm sick." She gags. She starts to cry. "Oh, Dad, this isn't good." She explains that she has been sick for a week now. She took a pregnancy test, and it came out positive. My knees buckle under the weight of my daughter's words, and I kneel, in prayer position, next to the toilet.

"Does your mother know about this?" I wipe spittle from her mouth with a warm, wet towel.

"No. Of course not! You can't tell her. Please."

"Who did this to you?"

"Dad," she says, holding her stomach.

"I want to know, Courtney."

"I always use protection, Dad. I promise." She begins to cry again. "Tell me."

"I think it was Kurt. But I don't know. I was really drunk at that party. But I..."

I hold her head on my shoulder. For one horrible moment, I imagine Kurt on top of my drunken daughter, a girl barely aware of her surroundings. She is telling me because she thinks that I am weak, that I will give in and let her vanish this dark secret with clinical magic. Madelyn would make her take responsibility and would never consent to the alternative to pregnancy.

In the mirror one morning, Mary Lou saw sand-yellow hair hanging over her face, covering one of her squinty green eyes. Country music twanged on the AM and she strummed her too-visible ribs like a guitar. Mary Lou poked her belly and it jiggled (she liked to call it her bar belly). Her fingers traced a kneecap, up along the loose flesh of a thin, bruised thigh, and into the smooth cup of a buttock.

In the mirror there was something missing, or maybe something extra, something that she no longer acknowledged. It did not occur to her that at the end of the day everything would be different, that she would be forever changed. It didn't need to. In her heart, the thing had already happened. It may not have been apparent to others, the people who gave her odd looks, but soon they, too, would recognize. She had expected this since she was a girl of seven looking over the edge of a carnival swimming pool.

Mary Lou took a bath as she did every morning since she could remember. She let her long hair float around her as she lay back in the tub. Her head half-submerged, she listened to her rings scrape the bottom of the fiberglass tub. She heard water splash in a clumsy rhythm around her body. Tropical bath salts soothed her skin that became so dry during the desert nights.

Before running errands, Mary Lou went to Elephant Butte Reservoir, not far behind her trailer. Such Saturdays were Mary

Lou's favorite days. She usually went looking for seashells and fossils in the desert hills near Elephant Butte. In warm weather she went to the reservoir and swam until her arms and legs were tired. Mary Lou floated on her back and watched the clouds slowly change form. She closed her eyes and imagined herself floating out of the reservoir and down the Rio Grande. She floated and floated until she reached the Gulf of Mexico. The waves took her far out into the ocean, and she rinsed her mouth with the saltwater before she dove into its depths. And then, a voice inside her said that she must be gone, for there were errands she needed to run.

I imagine the embryo growing inside Courtney as a fish, maybe a little like the Jesus fish with the Greek letters glued to the bumper of the Volvo. Does it know of itself? Does God know of or care for it? Does any of that really matter at this point, when what seems important to me is saving my daughter's future?

Mary Lou drove into town and stopped at the feed store. Inside, she filled out the paperwork to rent a log splitter. She hitched the splitter onto her El Camino and drove slowly back to her trailer. Mary Lou looked in the rearview mirror and saw the splitter bouncing up and down on the gravel that was her driveway. She drove around the trailer and then straight into a white, full-size bedsheet hanging from the clothesline. Looking out the windows, Mary Lou could only see the whiteness of this new tent and she felt, for a moment, as she did when Marty would press a pillow down onto her face as her thoughts fell back to the carnival. Mary Lou drove forward, stopped the car, and slid the shifter into park. She took a cinder block from her front steps to balance the weight of the log splitter, undid the hitch, and pulled the car back to the driveway.

The volunteer ambulance number was on a refrigerator magnet and she dialed, matter-of-factly explaining that she had had an accident. *She washed down a handful of painkillers with a tall glass of whiskey and went back outside with a sharp kitchen knife in her hand. With the knife, Mary Lou cut a long strip off the white sheet hanging on the clothesline. The log splitter started easily, and the smell of the gasoline-oil mix reminded her of men from the bar. Mary Lou walked over to the trailer and lifted another cinder block from the front steps. She hefted the concrete mass over to the splitter and set it on the steel I-beam, pushing the block up against the hydraulic arm. She pulled the lever that controlled the hydraulics. It slowly pushed the concrete block and she jerked the lever up when the block was about eight inches from the sharp wedge. Mary Lou then took the strip of sheet and with the painkillers overtaking her coordination, fumbled as she tried to tie it tightly around her right leg, high, at the top of her thigh. Straddling the I-beam, she leaned over so the top of her leg lay across it, and jerked the lever down.*

There was a gripping tightness that came from somewhere beyond her, and then released. Mary Lou fell on her back. With the last of her fading strength, she pushed herself up onto her elbows and looked down. There was blood, but it seemed so perfect. As she was about to lose conscientiousness, she heard the sirens calling her.

Courtney and I walk out of a downtown Planned Parenthood near where I often meet Mary Lou. We say nothing to each other, but I hold her hand as best I can. "I am the girl's father," I want to shout, for they all must think me some depraved individual who had impregnated a teenage girl. She cries the entire way home. Of course it is Courtney who suffers the most here, but I cannot help but feel like I have killed a part of myself.

I meet Mary Lou, and she tells me she would rather not go inside a hotel or a motel. Dog Boy has been sick and she doesn't want to leave him alone in the car.

"Let's drive to the sea," I say.

"There's no sea, Harold. Only plains and mountains."

"You don't want me to take you to the ocean?"

"There's not a lot of sense, Harold. I'm not a good swimmer."

We pull into the parking lot of Sloan's Lake, and I see the cross that sits up on the foothills. It's judging me again but this time not about my relationship with Mary Lou.

"Would you like a blowjob?"

"Not yet." I consider telling her about what happened with Courtney.

"Tell me something. Tell me a story."

"Harold, you know all the stories. You've heard all I got, baby"

"Tell me something, dammit. Say something. Anything. I'm giving you money." I pull my wallet out of my pants, take out all the bills, and throw them at her.

"I'll tell you something. There are no fucking mermaids! Got that? Not a single mermaid in the ocean and definitely none on the goddamn land."

"You're my mermaid, Mary Lou." I hear my voice as if I am deep underwater, sinking toward the bottom. It is the voice of a drowned man.

"I should have known you'd turn into a nut job. Look at me. I'm a woman. I'm no fish."

I rest my head on the steering wheel and begin to cry. The horn goes off and I lift my head to see a jogger giving me the finger.

"My baby girl was pregnant. And I helped her not be."

Mary Lou takes my hand from the steering wheel and holds it between her nicotine-stained fingers. She offers soft sounds of comfort and I sink into her like a babe in a mother's embrace.

The past three weeks, when the situation permits, Courtney comes into my office and I let her cry oceans of tears on my shoulder. She has taken to saying *Daddy* when she speaks to me. My heart aches when she says the word. I expected to gain an inner strength, though I have not; maybe I never will. I am truly a weak man, and dog food is my life. But Madelyn is stronger than I, and she harbors the fortitude to pull us all through. At the very least, she can pull Courtney through.

The kids are up in the mountains skiing, although I know Courtney will not ski, that she just wanted to get out of the house. I explained to her how we needed to tell her mother, how if Madelyn did not know, their relationship would never be the same. I didn't say how I was afraid of the responsibility that came with such a secret. My argument rested on the frail circle of naked honesty Father Winston preached. Not that I felt like the truth was a necessity, but that the weight of this truth was a large enough sack of rocks to sink me. Courtney consented reluctantly, but she didn't want to be there when I broke the news.

"Madelyn, we need to talk."

"Make it quick, Harold. I'm off to buy new drapes." She is measuring the windows. "We need something darker," she says, as if she has heard me. "The neighbors can see right through these."

"You might want to sit down."

"Harold, can't you see I'm busy."

I would like her to sit, to listen to me, but she won't. "Your daughter, our daughter. Courtney was pregnant."

Madelyn drops her tape measure and stares back at me. Her chin shakes in terror, but her eyes pierce me with harpoons of hate and blame. "What do you mean?'

"She is not pregnant anymore."

"Why didn't anyone tell me? Did she have a miscarriage?" She begins to gasp for air. "Just what the hell is going on here, Harold?"

"No. She did not have a miscarriage, Madelyn."

Her howl cuts through me, shears me to the core, and I look down to see my guts on the floor. She screams, starts tearing down the drapes, and screams. I walk up behind my wife and put my hand to the back of her head to try to feel where the strength will come from. I grasp her arm and pull her to me.

"I'm sorry," I say, thinking that I have finally forgiven her.

Madelyn tries to shake me off, but I stay there, listening to her mutter prayers so quickly it sounds like water over stones. She says, "You should have told me, you should have told me, you should have told me."

Back when there was hope for James, I invested a good deal of money in a college fund. I decide to close the account and absorb the penalties for early withdrawal. I have with me a glass milk bottle. I drive to Sloan's Lake with the money, rolled-up hundred-dollar bills, and place them inside. I've never built one of those ships inside a bottle, but you could buy a real ship with the cash that is inside this one. I drive, and Mary Lou is exactly where I thought she would be, hobbling on her crutches with Dog Boy at her side. I pull the car over and Mary Lou leans inside.

"Harold, I was wondering if I would see you again." She smiles, looks genuinely glad to see me, and begins to open the door.

I pull the handle back, trying to close the door, but it is left ajar. "I can't stay, but I have something for you," I say, handing her a brown paper bag with the bottle inside.

"Bath salts?" she says, taking the bag.

"Whatever you want it to be. Take care, Mary Lou."

"Bye, Harold."

I pull away from the curb but before driving a block must stop at a red light. In my rearview mirror, I see Mary Lou peer into the bag and then quickly shut it. She looks around her and then looks back at my car. I honk the horn, and when the light turns green I drive away.

I walk out into the water until it is up to my knees. "Come on!" I say. "Come on out! The water is brilliant." The ocean is warm and the waves are choppy. They crash against the backs of my knees, making me feel awkward and vulnerable. My balance isn't the best.

James walks down the beach, obviously embarrassed by my tourist show of exuberance. He will be gone for some time and will return with red eyes and in a somber mood. He'll say that he was swimming with his eyes open, but his hair will be dry.

Courtney and Madelyn stand at the edge of the Atlantic Ocean with toes in the water, and they back up with each incoming wave. Their mouths move, but I cannot make out what they are saying. I turn my back to them and walk out a little farther before I dive in and swim a few weak strokes.

Courtney leaves her mother behind and makes her way out to me. Without saying a word she dives in, and I feel something against my foot and then her hand on my ankle. In a few seconds her head and shoulders break the surface, and she is a good thirty feet beyond me.

Madelyn does not swim out, but she walks slowly and rises on her tiptoes with each wave. She is standing next to me, and a shiver passes through her goosed skin. She looks good in her new bathing suit, and I know that tonight her skin will be red with warmth and tender to the touch. Madelyn waves to Courtney with one hand and beneath the water her other grasps mine. With her hand in mine, I spin the ring on her finger and watch my daughter swim.

TO THY SPEED ADD WINGS

AS WAS HIS PRACTICE OF TWO MONTHS, at precisely 10:00 a.m. Donald Mota shuffled across the false balcony that stretched across the second floor of his mansion. He was dressed, as always, in khaki shirt and pants, accessorized with a silk ascot. His intent was to observe his accountant, Joanie, while she used the toilet during her coffee break. Donald lived on the third floor, and the first and second floors had been renovated into the offices and classrooms of the institution of higher learning that he had founded. The sandstone was February-cold against the paper of his eighty-five-year-old skin. Two months prior his wife had died, leaving him lonely and lustful, despite his equipment not having been fully functional for a decade. No matter. Sometime around Watergate, his wife had replaced his apparatus with an electric back and foot massager. Such were the ways of progress.

Donald stretched until he was peering from the side of the window and could see Joanie pulling up her skirt and sitting upon the commode. Though cigarettes had given Joanie's face the texture and color of an overripe cantaloupe, her hair was wavy and lustrous. When Joanie and Donald studied the account ledgers he would lean over her shoulder, yearning to lose himself, louse-like, in her bouffant. He had founded the Nat Mota School in 1969, naming it after his father. For over two decades the pencil pushers at the IRS had kept a careful tally of his tax indiscretions, but near the turn of the century he had the sense and good fortune to hire Joanie. The IRS hadn't knocked on his door in fifteen years. Having too much respect for Joanie's artful manipulation of numbers, he had never attempted to lay a hand on her. Donald watched as Joanie turned away to reach for the toilet paper, one cheek lifting from the seat to reveal the soft white curd of her derrière. He loosed his grip on the railing and in benediction touched a single finger first to his silk ascot and then to the windowpane. Such woe: Donald Mota, a man without a friend to whom he was not also employer.

In that bittersweet moment, Donald heard what he thought was machine-gun fire, and he lost his balance. He toppled over the railing but not before locking eyes with Joanie, her face holed in a scream. Falling two stories, he batted the air uselessly, attempting to cling to Joanie's siren sound, which happened to be percussed by the *rat-a-tat-tat* of a woodpecker beating its mating call against a rain gutter.

Thank God, he thought, this fall is not long enough for my life to flash before my eyes. I devoted everything to my country and to education. And now I am reduced to voyeur, a peeping Tom, and a clumsy one at that.

Young and virile, I shipped to Korea with the 2nd Infantry Division, Sergeant Donald Mota. When the 2nd was decimated by the Chinese near Kunu-ri, I was hit by shrapnel and came to without my squad, my socks, or my boots. I hid and scurried for days, a rat on two bloodied paws. The sun rising on the Kaechon River, I stumbled upon a sleeping giant of a Korean soldier. With a rock the size of a softball, I brained him dead. Eight minutes later, medics from the 2nd found me fifty yards from my kill, sitting behind a tree and lacing my stolen boots. Only when I realized that I had been in UN territory the entire time and that I had killed to obtain shoes that I wore for less than an hour, did I feel regret.

I returned to Fort Logan and trained recruits to hate the enemy. Not a hard task. You just show them the right way to look into a mirror. Nightly, the Korean giant would visit me in my dreams, whispering sweet nothings: *Kunu-ri, Kunu-ri.*

—

This falling seems tedious, Donald thought. Joanie's scream echoed across the campus. When he hit the spruce hedges below the false balcony, the air went out of him. He remembered his wife, Anita, dying, her eye whites yellowed and tired, and he thought, good God, I'm still breathing.

The early sixties had offered nothing but promise and we were filled with the verve to milk it. After the war, I had taken a speed-reading class with famed Mormon Evelyn Wood. I wanted to know everything. I became a concert promoter. I got The Beatles to Red Rocks in '64 and later booked Led Zeppelin's first American show. I didn't so much favor the music as I did the profits and power of mass appeal.

Anita drove drag races—funny cars—out at Bandimere Speedway, hers a turquoise GTO she christened Gypsy. She was the most eligible bachelorette in the Rocky Mountain region and grown men would do backflips just to see her bat an eyelid. I drove a '58 Maserati, the fastest car on the Valley Highway, and I was liberal with Father's money. Before I proposed, Anita and I sat in front of the fireplace and she watched me read Ayn Rand's *Atlas Shrugged* in three hours. I wanted to show her that I was capable of deep thoughts.

The wedding took place in my Cadillac at one-hundred-twenty-five miles an hour, the minister and witnesses in the backseat. Sitting on my lap, Anita steered while we blasted Herb Alpert & the Tijuana Brass at such a high volume that we needed to scream our vows, and even then our promises went unheard.

Anita hit the national racing circuit. Her pit crew was untouchable. After winning the Rocky Flats Cup, Anita sprayed champagne on the boys, a wry smile on her face. Her humor was not lost on me. Axel Maxime, a Frenchman who was her lead mechanic, sidled up close to me and whispered, "With Anita, it's like swimming, no?" He sniffed his grease-stained fingers and raised his eyebrows. He wore an impeccably groomed mustache.

"Back to France with you, grease monkey!" I said. I might have punched him had he not had the advantage of superior strength.

With Anita, the smells of gasoline and burning tire rubber were aphrodisiacs. Riding her from behind one Easter morning, I spied smudged handprints on her hips. I slowed my pace and said, "Did you disgrace our marriage with a member of your pit crew?"

"Harder!" she cried, slapping at me.

"With a wrench-head frog-eater?"

"You spend all your time in concert halls, schmoozing in the green room with groupies and hippies. When you come home, all you want to do is read!"

I had terrible insomnia in those days, and exercise only made it worse. "True, but I have never strayed."

She pretended not to hear. She was insatiable. I was beyond release.

After a week of spying and scheming, I knew Maxime's routine, that every morning he jogged a particular country road. At daybreak, I drove the Maserati to that very location and ran him over dead. I buried him in an abandoned silver mine on one of Father's properties, and then, wearing Anita's crash helmet, I piloted the Maserati straight into a mud- and rock-filled ditch. I totaled my beloved, but all the evidential mess of blood and hair was vanished into the ground.

Anita hired other mechanics, but no one had Maxime's touch. I felt no pride in the thing, no sense that honor had been restored. Maxime had given my wife the thing she wanted most—the glory of speed—and I took it away in a jealous panic. She never suspected a thing and in our marriage bed we were active, though mournful. Soon, she gave birth to a son she named Ryan. The first time I saw his face, I knew he was not of my seed. I had killed Maxime, and nine months later Anita had resurrected him.

—

Donald woke in a blanket of pain and haze. His left arm in a cast, he reached with his right to feel where his aching head should have been and found nothing but gauze and tape. It was not the first time he had awoken in the hospital. In the last ten years, he had had two heart attacks, a seizure while swimming laps, and just before Anita died of pancreatic cancer, he suffered a stroke that left half his face looking underinflated. At what point exactly had his body committed mutiny? To hell with it, he thought. To the light, Donald! Go to the light. Forget this mortal coil, its double toil and trouble.

"Mr. Mota, can you hear me?"

"My head is killing me."

"You had a nasty fall, sir."

It all came rushing back to him—the curve of Joanie's posterior, the machine-gun report of the woodpecker's beak, and Joanie's anguished scream. He fell back to his pillow and bellowed.

"You can thank your lucky stars for the shrubbery," the nurse said.

"Lucky stars? I should have had those things removed years ago," Donald said.

"Your daughters were here earlier, sir."

"Add insult to injury," Donald said. He and Anita had six daughters, each dumber and meaner than the last. The boy Anita conceived with Maxime was the only child to amount to anything. He was in real estate and horses. Hitting the morphine drip, Donald cursed death. Why do you come so slowly, ravaging my body piecemeal? Perhaps I should have driven the Maserati off the cliff rather than run down old Maxime? Done it with one resolute foot to the floor.

In the spring of '69, Father demanded that I get out of the concert-promotion business. The old man knew his stuff—he had been a missionary, a rancher, and a first-rate capitalist with holdings in oil, minerals, and chemicals. *A church or school, that's the ticket*, he said. My tastes were too fast for religion. Seeing that I had been a motivational specialist in the army and given my interest in speed-reading, a school seemed the proper choice. I drove to Salt Lake City and consulted with Evelyn Wood. We shared a desire to change the world for the better. Her motivation came from pure generosity, mine from guilt. I returned to Denver and for my final gig I promoted the Denver Pop Festival, which featured Jimi Hendrix playing for the last time with The Experience. There were clashes between the police and so-called peace activists. Tear gas, rocks, bottles. Flower power had run its course and withered on the vine.

The spring of 1970, radical leftists abducted Father from the mansion. They hadn't expected Anita to be in the house, so they bound her to an oversized Remington replica Father had sitting in the garden. Before they left, they kicked her a couple of times and proceeded to say unpleasant things about her anatomy and her social class. They asked for a ridiculous ransom that we refused to pay, and they gunned down Father while he sat upon the toilet. Crapped on the crapper at the ripe old age of ninety.

I was a wreck. Hungover by day, blind drunk by night. The whole mess skewed my judgment. With a slice of my inheritance, I bought Anita and myself matching gold Maserati Ghibli SS Coupes. I had visions of us street racing away our pain. Anita, traumatized, soon quit drag racing and got hired at UPS as a delivery driver. While she looked good in the shorts, it was obvious that she had lost her fire. She cut her hair short and spent her time packing the children's lunchboxes and knotting herself mindless with macramé projects. She lost interest in all matters carnal, and she developed what Donald thought was an unhealthy interest in her son.

In 1976, while at a speed-reading conference in Abeline,

Kansas, Evelyn Wood and I toured the Eisenhower Library. Granted special access to the archives, we read feverishly. Although she was sixty-seven, nearly twenty years my senior, she enchanted me. We made love beneath Ike's portrait, and what I initially thought was Evelyn's climax was actually a stroke. I feared for her life and hollered for help. Security arrived before I had the chance to find her panties or pull up my pants. It was in all of the papers. They kicked poor Evelyn out of the Tabernacle Choir, though the stroke did such damage I don't think she was much for singing. Evelyn's husband filed a lawsuit claiming that I stole their speed-reading techniques. They won a pittance.

Anita found discovered my transgression while checking out at the supermarket and perusing the tabloids. She demanded a second house in Golden. Even when we slept under the same roof, we kept separate beds. Publicly shamed, I had no one to whom I needed to answer. I devoted all of my time to the school. I was a parasite upon my dead father's fortune.

One night after I burned a fish dinner for one, I called Anita. "I know the secret you've been keeping. I see Maxime's Frenchy features in the boy's face."

"I would divorce you if I did not think it was the very thing you desired," she said.

It was not my desire, dearest. Does this mean I won?

"What in God's name were you doing on the false balcony?"

Donald stared at his daughter, Pamela, the youngest and dimmest of the six dim bulbs that were, unexplainably, he and Anita's offspring. "Never mind that!" Donald slumped back against the pillow. He hit the morphine drip, resisting a double dose. Who knew what kind of business he had ahead of himself?

"What have you heard from Joanie?" He hated to involve Pamela, dumb as she was, but he had no one else whom he could trust.

"She's tenured her resignation!"

"*Tendered*, you boor!" While Anita was dying, Pamela spent her days poking around and affixing little stickers to the bottom of things she desired once her mother was dead. Anita had always claimed that Donald was too hard on Pamela, but he saw her for the vindictive and greedy carp that she was.

Every item in the house with a sticker Donald had pitched into the trash.

Pamela stood before him now, waving about an envelope. "She claims that you were watching her when she was in the ladies' room."

"Just read me the letter."

February 13, 2014

Dear Mr. Mota,

While I have undergone various indignities these last fifteen years, I did not suspect that you would have the audacity to watch me during such a private moment. I have never in my life been so humiliated, and while I do value the years I spent in service at the Nat Mota School, I am afraid that I need to submit my resignation, effective immediately.
Yours Respectfully,
Joanie Alexander
P.S.
You'll find your claim tickets for your dry cleaning in the upper right-hand drawer of my desk. In the left-hand drawer, you'll find a list of instructions and to-dos for my replacement.

"Yours," he whispered. The words on the page were an anvil dropped on his scarred heart. All those years with Anita, their love life as passionless as the passing of gas or the blowing of a nose, the charm of reflex.

Yours, Joanie wrote. Maybe there was more to senior citizenry than diapers and degradation. He was consumed with her handwriting. The hourglass of her eights. The zeroes with the belt cinched across the middle. Her fives with the perfectly curved bottom. He thought, Take me now, God. If you let me live, I will accept it as a sign. Otherwise, let me die.

When he opened his eyes, Pamela was still sitting at his side, pinching her chin in that way she did when attempting deep thought. "Do you think that Joanie might, you know, tell someone about the books?" Pamela was lazy in habit and mind, but, to her credit, she had a mean streak that provided her best thinking. "We should probably start burning records."

"Get my khakis and ascot," he said.

A block from the mansion, Donald spied the police cars that he knew were accompanying IRS agents. His pain was overwhelming. Fifteen years. He remembered when Joanie first walked through the door, a newly minted masters in accounting from Regis University in hand. She was Catholic, and fifteen years later was an underpaid spinster. He realized that he knew nothing of her home life. A spinster. Good God. If nothing else, he owed her an apology. For once, he would do the right thing.

"That bitch," Pamela said. "After we employ her fifteen years, this is how she treats us?"

"Do what you can to keep them from going upstairs," he said.

"I'll call the lawyer."

"Call all of them," Donald said. He opened the door and limped away, feeling in his pocket for the keys to the one Maserati Ghibli (Anita's) that was still operational.

"Where do you think you're going?"

"Do what I ask, Pamela. I beg."

There were two vehicles in Joanie's driveway. The blue Nissan he recognized. It was a rust bucket. He tried to remember when she drove something else, but he could not. He would replace it. If she wanted he would buy her a Cadillac, though he hoped she would want nothing more than a used Japanese compact. No, no, he thought; give her whatever it is that she desires.

He limped across the driveway, brushing from his khaki shirt and pants the debris that remained from his fall. He knocked on the door and a stout, chiseled-chin man answered. "Joanie!" Donald called, standing on his tiptoes to see over the behemoth.

"Who are you?" barrel-chest said.

"I'm her employer, you oaf!"

"Harvey, who is it?"

"I've come to beg for your forgiveness, Joanie. I've been an awful cad." Donald ducked beneath the behemoth's arm, falling in the process, but landing on his back so as not to reinjure his arm. Still, he cried out in pain. He scuttled across the living room floor, where sitting on a recliner made for two—*Dear Jesus, I cannot think of this as a loveseat*—was his Joanie. A box of Valentine's candy sat on the coffee table. He stood and stared at the box in disbelief.

"Candy?" Joanie said.

A thick finger poked at his back and Donald dropped to his knees. He felt a great and profound pain in his chest. He lost his desire to apologize. He wanted to sing out in exaltation. "Oh, Joanie. All these years and only now do I have the courage to tell you the way I feel."

"This is the peeping Tom?" the man said.

Joanie muttered an affirmative.

"Why are you in my house?" Joanie pressed the lever on the chair and sprung forward. They were watching drag racing of all things. Donald's heart dropped. "Your house?" he said to the man, though he still faced Joanie. Her face, the O punched in the middle like there had been the biggest of misunderstandings.

Donald crawled to the dual recliners and attempted to lift himself. He didn't have the strength. "These years," Donald said. He tried to speak but the words, the energy, where had it all gone? He felt a fist in the back of his head and it was as if his heart seized. He clutched at his chest and fell again onto his back.

Miraculously, he was now positioned such that he could see directly up Joanie's skirt. She was wearing underwear he had never seen before, thin cut. A thong, is that what they called it? Oh, how he longed to reach for her. So many things he had to say. *Dearest Joanie!* his heart screamed. *All these years and you cooking the books, never saying a word. My love, my life.*

Joanie stood next to the giant. From the floor, Donald started to look up her dress but then was struck by the sight of her shoes, a pair of slip-on casuals that he remembered on Anita's feet. She had gone through her things before she died, giving away items of no real value to friends and employees. Still, it drove Pamela batty.

From the television he heard the cars, pre-race, burning rubber, the revving of the dreadfully powerful engines. From between Joanie's feet, he saw the Maserati Ghibli in all its golden splendor.

How many years had it been since the Maseratis had been delivered to their driveway? And she never drove the thing, not once, even went so far as to say that it was despicable to spend Nat's money that way after his murder. You were wrong, Anita, Donald thought. You were wrong and had you driven that car, had we raced each other up and down the canyon roads, we would have survived. We would have loved until the end. She had once threatened to give the car to her son, but it was Donald's name on the title and he had refused to sign it over. After Anita's death he changed his will, giving almost everything to the child that was not his own, one pitiful gesture that he hoped she would somehow understand, wherever she might be.

Something shifted and the gold paint on the car shimmered. Anita stepped out. She was wearing her racing uniform and she held out her hand. Donald's eyes closed. Then he was walking to her. His first and last love. There were two Maseratis in the driveway.

Joanie stared down at Donald Mota. His body released a sound like a sigh, as if some great weight had been lifted.

GHOST IMAGE

GINNY STUART WATCHED EASTON ALBION as he stared at her televised image. Presented in electromagnetic waves, Ginny was *live*, and yet she herself—her body—sat ten feet from him. Easton breathed deeply and focused on the televised Ginny, as if her image was holy and her body was incidental, or at best, a relic. Ginny stood and walked behind Easton, who now also appeared on the screen. She touched his shoulder and he closed his eyes. "I wish you'd at least let me sing, or dance, or *something.*"

"You're dancing between the past and the now, Ginny. You're an apparition and you're real. I like you between two worlds."

Ginny smiled into the camera, uncertain of what else to do or think about what she considered Easton's film experiment for wayward youth. After running away from home three days ago, she had arrived in Denver's industrial gut at the once-abandoned flourmill—the Affiliate—where Easton's crew squatted. She was both repelled by and attracted to Easton, and though the other kids had been friendly enough, she didn't leave Easton's side. The television news called people like Easton *charismatic.* The flourmill was abuzz with the energy and pretense of filming, along with the laziness of watching the end product. The activity reminded her of life at the horse track, the cycle of preparation, the importance of performance. During times like these, kicking back in front of the TVs, the track broke into her thoughts— horse hooves pounding the dirt, her mother's equine scent, the announcer's English accent and the hot wind whispering through the pages of a trashy magazine as she sat in a chaise longue in the sun.

By chance she had met Easton at a local reservoir the summer before, and she thought him strange, the way he spoke about the flight patterns of birds and how they resembled the configuration of a soul in the process of transmigration. He looked at her as if she were an avian species he had discovered. Their afternoon together hadn't been romantic but the day was filled with ways of seeing that she had never imagined. She had enjoyed the way he didn't talk down to her, as if he expected her to understand all of his theories and have some of her own. She ended up here because there was nowhere else to turn. Her Uncle Charlie was a Denver cop, and while she liked him, his being a cop eliminated him as an option.

Although bright outside, shadows sprawled across the floor in haunted black planes, intersecting line segments and rays. Within this abstract geometry sat the cast and crew, who were mostly high-school age, labeled runaways and castaways, rejects and retards. Sprawled out on the floor or moving cameras and adjusting pictures and sound, they were a scarred lot—suburban exiles, urban eccentrics—adorned with safety pins, homemade tattoos, scabbed skateboard knees and elbows, all worn like hieroglyphics on flesh walls. Three days amongst these kids and Ginny was convinced that she should go home. She missed her brother, Bobby, and though she wouldn't have thought it possible, she missed her mother, too.

Ginny had been watching herself all morning, both live on tape and in footage from the last few days. At the track her life had no purpose, as if she had been disappearing, but now she had reappeared, and here was the taped evidence. Televisions lined the walls, older models—black-and-whites, consoles, small portables—most with fuzzy pictures. Images crackled across the screens and the sounds created a cacophony reminiscent of the track clubhouse. She had no clue what any of it meant.

The Affiliate reeked of cat piss and thus far Ginny's diet consisted of canned peaches and expired cinnamon buns. The first day, she had been frightened. "Every time one of you homeless wannabes shows up," Easton had said, "you jeopardize this whole enterprise. Don't you realize that when your mom reports you MIA, the cops will look here?" Easton pleaded with his eyes, big and blinking and comprised of two distinct hues of blue. "This isn't some vacation you return from and then tell your friends about." He had grabbed her arm then but noticed a green bruise just above her elbow and quickly let go, as if he himself was injured. "Three days, and then you'll decide." He never asked why she left home, so she didn't tell him about her mother—Janice Stuart, the horse trainer—who possessed barn-cultivated strength. Ginny wanted sanctuary, not his pity, which flowed from some reservoir so deep that she couldn't fathom. She had left home with nothing but a change of clothes, $27.89, and a debit card—with fifty dollars in the account—that her mother gave her three years ago expressly for emergencies. Knowing that it could be used to track her, she had ditched her cell phone.

Running away and living on the streets seemed the best way to take revenge. She did not quite remember her father, though his absence was palpable. Her mother had told her that he was an alcoholic and acid casualty who, unable to keep a job, had abandoned the family for the streets. When she was ten, her father had been shot and killed. Her Uncle Charlie had been one of the officers on the scene.

Easton sat cross-legged on a dirty pink blanket, facing four televisions that sat stacked in a corner of the room. On one screen flickered an image of the flourmill's exterior, seven stories of nearly gutted cement and steel carcass. Even though it was summer, large flakes of electronic snow fell on the flourmill. While he watched the sets simultaneously, Easton paid special attention to the black-and-white television to the far right, which showed Ginny *live on tape*. He could have turned ninety degrees to his right and looked directly at her—the *physical* Ginny—but her television self had more appeal. The camera was mounted on top of the television and he had a frontal view of her face only when she, too, confronted her black-and-white image, which she now did. Her hair was gray, straight, parted in the middle, a narrow, coffin-like frame around her thin face.

Easton pulled his eyes from the televisions, leaned back on his palms, and stared at the ceiling. He wore cutoff khakis and no shirt, his chest thin and pale. Tipping his head back as far as his neck would allow, he closed his eyes and sighed. "Fischer," he said.

From the other side of the room a guy with a mane of curly dark hair walked up behind Easton. "Yo!"

"I'd like to talk with Ginny." Easton's voice was thin but commanding and, in the concrete hollows of the flourmill, seemed to come in surround sound.

"Gotcha," Fischer said. He walked to the black-and-white set and detached the camera from its mount. "Rolling!" Fischer said.

"I'm right here, Easton," Ginny said.

Fischer panned the camera from Ginny to Easton as each spoke. Easton continued to stare at the snowy profile of her image. Easton's skin was like celluloid, yellowed and semi-translucent, as if focused light could pass through him and project upon a screen. "I know where you are," he said.

"So look!"

"I'm looking at you transformed. I'm looking at your *soul*, Ginny."

"You should make me a star," Ginny said.

"A celestial object?"

"A supernova."

"A flash in eternity?"

Ginny shook her head and looked at the TV, at Easton. He smiled at her and then she witnessed her own tight-lipped smirk. When she read her magazines at the horse track, Ginny often imagined herself a writer, a model, or a musician, in some non-occupation where people paid attention to her and smiled at what they saw. Easton's operation didn't really meet her expectations for celebrity. They didn't even show the films to anyone but themselves. Still, she could tell that he was star-struck by her. She didn't know why, and frankly she didn't care.

"All the televisions at the track show dogs and horses," Ginny said. "At the trailer, we can get Channel 35, and the day after it rains Channel 6 sorta comes in."

"My father only let me watch CNN until I was ten. It's the death channel, but most of them are." Easton looked beyond Ginny, rather than at her, and smiled. "The death of the body is a repackaging, a transformation. I believe in mixing the corporeal and spiritual works of mercy, though I'm no Catholic. To bury the dead, you must first comfort their souls. I want you to know what you're getting yourself into."

"You talk like a televangelist."

Ginny thought of home. Was she burying her past? Could she just leave and never return? She wanted to tell Easton that she was scared, but that would mean admitting that she didn't understand his word puzzles, the endless taping, that she didn't understand him. Even if she was confused she wanted to get lost in his mystery, and she thought that if she didn't say the wrong thing he too would find her mysterious, would listen to all of her silly little secrets rather than stare at her on the televisions.

"Tonight, you'll need to go out and dive."

"Dumpster dive?" The others had told her about the alley trips.

"I'll go with you," Easton said. "Fischer will film. You and me with backpacks, flashlights and gloves, Ginny."

"How could a girl pass something like that up?"

"After, we'll pay a visit to the passing; we'll send them a word of encouragement." Easton held a newspaper obituary and pointed to a circled entry.

"I can't tell if you're creepy or just really, really funny."

"I know." Like lunar acne, static pocked her televised skin. A cat meowed. Ginny laced her fingers in front of her face, lowered her hands and bit her lip, all while a horizontal black line rose from the bottom of the screen, rolled to the top, and then dropped back down, cutting through her eyes. No one moved or said anything for five, ten, fifteen seconds. The black line rose again and fell to the bottom of the screen, disappearing into an abyss that none of them could see. "That," Easton said, "was beautiful."

Ginny found herself giggling, though she hadn't done a thing.

Homeschooled out of a camping trailer, Ginny and Bobby only knew life on the back side of the track—trainers, agents, jockeys, stable hands, and Mexican cowboys. Ginny's mother trained thoroughbred horses at low-class tracks, and like nomads or carnies they traveled from Arizona to Colorado to New Mexico. Ginny had spent most of her seventeen years on the circuit, not what she would have requested for a childhood, but it was okay, it was hers. When she was younger and they didn't travel as much, during the summer—the season of county and state fairs—her mother entered her in talent shows, lip-synching contests mostly. Ginny choreographed her own dance routines and she was good, the blue ribbons hanging from the trailer walls proving it. Ginny loved to sing, even when she only mouthed the words. "Wild Horses," "A Horse with No Name," "Back in the Saddle." She knew all the great horse songs.

Every race day at Arapahoe Park, Ginny had sat in front of the televisions in the grandstand and watched the English announcer's pre-race show. In a manner approaching the mystical, he had handicapped the outcomes. Ginny rarely stayed for the races themselves and when she had told the announcer this at a jockey's wedding he had whispered a prediction in her ear. The announcer hadn't predicted that Ginny's mother would later witness the kiss, the hand beneath Ginny's blouse, nor the hand up her skirt. Her mother walked up, shoved the announcer, and dragged Ginny away. She didn't say a word until they reached the trailer, and then she beat Ginny as if she were breaking a stubborn, or stupid, horse.

"I already have no fucking idea where we are," Ginny said. They stood on a sidewalk near downtown, where the houses mingled with mansions converted to apartment buildings, where the elegance of the past had been split into crowded quarters for the present poor.

"You're right *here*," Easton said.

"And here," Fischer said. He tapped the camera in front of his face.

Easton pointed to an alley and for the first time since they had left the Affiliate, they strayed from the sidewalk. Easton could spend the entire day immobile in front of the TV, staring in his singular and bizarre reverence, but once in action, he moved fast. He reminded her of her favorite horses, the ones who in the paddock stood with their heads low, as if in meditation, but once the starting gate opened, unleashed a flurry of speed. Ginny's feet hurt from trying to keep up. Easton turned and handed Ginny a pair of leather gloves. "Lots of dope in this neighborhood, and you don't want to get stuck." Easton threw back the plastic lid of the dumpster. "We scavenge light. Only what we can fit in here and here." Easton slapped their backpacks. "No food. No appliances. Small things we can flip for cash or use at the Affiliate."

Streetlights radiated the alley with sickly green light, while the shadows of trees and cobwebbed wires carved undecipherable symbols on the concrete. Ginny leaned her head over the rim of the dumpster and looked at the remains of people, all the lost footage.

Earlier, after they left the Affiliate, Ginny had called Bobby. He sounded scared when he heard her voice, but once she had assured him that she was safe, he had said she was going to be in deep, deep shit. "What the hell were you thinking, kissing Steve?" *Bobby.* "I mean, come on, he's one of Mom's boyfriends." *Her stable of boyfriends.* Bobby laughed. *If I got to choose between you telling Mom or not, which do you think I would choose?* Bobby was silent for a moment. "If you promise to call back tomorrow," he said, "I'll make the choice *you* want." *Yes.* "And the day after?" *Bobby.* They based their sibling love on agreeing to disagree and on cutting deals.

"Dig in," Easton said. He tore open a garbage bag, picking through the contents—rotten food, empty beer cans, envelopes. "Bingo." He flipped through a stack of magazines. "This is good and bad. Porn sells, but it's heavy." He held up three copies of *Juggs,* unzipped Ginny's pack, and shoved them inside.

"They're heavy, so I carry them?" Easton shrugged and grinned. Ginny tore open a plastic carcass and even though she smelled nothing foul, she wrinkled her nose. "I have no idea what I'm looking for."

Behind the camera, Fischer laughed. Easton walked to the other side of the dumpster and opened the lid. "This is re-run garbage." He pointed to the shredded bags. "Someone's beat us to it." A rat ran under the dumpster. Ginny jumped and feigned fright, even though she saw plenty of rats at the track. She bit her lip for the camera. Easton shook his head. "Bad acting. There's no second takes here."

The next dumpster lid was propped open, a giant, mutated clam bursting with boxes and bags piled high, a coffee table stuck out like a tongue. Fischer zoomed in on Ginny, the camera only inches from her face. She tilted her chin down, pursed her lips, and winked. She ripped open a bag, pawing its contents—bills, banana peels, bread bags. She held up each item as she imagined they would in old-fashioned magazine ads. If her mother saw her now, she would freak. She would freak, beat her, freak again. And Bobby? Bobby would laugh, call her a bag lady, and then ask how much money she got for the goods. She found a blue plastic box the size of a dictionary. "Is this anything?" A sticker with a red cross was glued to the center of the box.

Easton popped the lid and surveyed the contents. "This, Ginny, is good." Band-Aids, ibuprofen, bar soap. Easton sifted through the same bag that had held the first-aid kit. "And this, dear girl, is gold." He held up three prescription bottles—pain reliever with codeine, neomycin, and sulfonamide.

"You'll scavenge prescription drugs when you have no idea what they are?" Ginny said. She opened her backpack.

"But I do know what they are. I'm not only a film director. I also happen to be a street doctor."

"Licensed and certified, too, I bet."

By unrecognized authorities. You go to a hospital as a runaway and, well, you're back home, pronto. I treat those *beyond* modern medical care."

"You're the patron saint of the garbage dumpster."

Easton grinned, and for the first time she noticed that his teeth seemed too small for his mouth. Even with this defect, he was lovely in his eeriness, like a picture of Billy the Kid she had once seen on a T-shirt. Headlights filled the alley. "Move!" he said. Fischer ran backward with the camera pointed at Easton, Ginny, and the car behind them. Ginny saw the silhouette of the unlit rollers. Cops. Fischer led them down a side street, up a small hill, and back into another alley.

When they stopped, out of breath, Easton gave Ginny a sharp look, as if trying to read something in her eyes. "We weren't doing anything wrong," he said. "But the meds aren't cool. They would have checked the bags. And you, of course, are definitely listed as MIA."

"Where are we?" Ginny stared into the camera, feeling like she was rehearsing a tired line. She turned her head, picturing the image of her entire face. She thought about how Easton would watch her tomorrow.

Fischer stepped back, panned the camera up and down the

street of large Victorians and regal neo-colonials. "No use diving here," Easton said. "They've got no dumpsters, but they do have excellent stages."

Ginny looked at the bay windows, the towering black fences, and thought of the trailer she had been living in, her bed that folded down from the wall. The security systems in these palaces cost more than any home her mother had ever owned. Ginny felt criminal, small, and envious. Although past midnight, inside the Victorian she saw a woman sitting at a table with a ceramic bowl of yellow bananas, red apples, and green pears. *A bowl of fucking fruit.* The very idea seemed stupid, completely ridiculous. Didn't they put their fruit in the refrigerator? And then it occurred to her that the house was most certainly air-conditioned. Something clicked and hatred replaced her jealousy. That stupid woman with her professionally styled hair and her air-conditioned fruit. If the woman had kids Ginny's age, they probably vacationed in Europe, were lifeguards, and went to pool parties where they ingested designer drugs.

Ginny caught Easton staring at her, his found species, a never-before-seen bird. She wondered if Easton had arisen from the pages of a book, or better yet, stepped out of a movie. He reached out and took her hand. "Ready for some real fun?" They walked a few blocks, the houses growing smaller, but still lavish by Ginny's standards. They cut through an alley and Easton paused. A large sandstone stood in front of them. He pulled out a piece of folded newsprint from his pocket. He unfolded it and smiled at Fischer. "You've got wonderful instincts, Fishy."

"Not this again." Fischer lowered his camera. "I think this sucks."

"Hey! We're rolling here."

Fischer turned the camera lens toward his own face. "For the record, I think this is a bad idea."

"But for a time, I went to school here," Easton said, his voice almost pleading. Easton walked up the house's driveway, and Ginny thought that the windows looked like abandoned mines.

He beckoned over his shoulder for them to follow. When they caught up, he stood at a side door, pressed against it like a lover, and jimmied its lock. "Open says me." Easton turned the knob and slowly swung open the door and whispered, "Cellar door, cellar door, cellar door."

"I thought the idea was to be low-key, to *not* attract attention," Ginny said.

Easton grabbed her hand and walked inside, his flashlight illuminating a finished basement, plush carpet, couches, and an entertainment center. A bar. He handed his flashlight to Fischer and removed Ginny's own flashlight from her bag. "We'll need extra light in here, Fischer." Fischer took the flashlights, found a table, and lit the makeshift stage. "Donald Mota, we know you are here, that your spirit walks without its former body."

"This is a dead man's house?" Ginny said. She pulled her hand from the table she had been leaning against, as if the deceased's possessions held the essence of death itself. "Gross."

"Don't be afraid, Donald." Easton turned slowly in a circle and then held his arms out to Ginny. "Let's dance."

"There's no music," Ginny said. She stood with her hands on her hips.

"There's music inside. Listen." He placed his ear to her chest, grabbed her hand, and swayed back and forth. "Electric slide." He let go of her hand, took a few steps forward, and then slid to his left.

"That's not the electric slide. Watch." The announcer had taught Ginny the dance at the jockey's wedding. She thought it had been innocent fun. Ginny slid her leg out and then the rest of her body followed, as if pulled by a rope. Easton stood to her side, mimicking her steps. They laughed. He grabbed her by the waist, and their midsections created an easy friction.

"This is what I mean. You hear the music. Dancing will ease the pain."

Ginny didn't know if he meant her pain or the dead man's.

In a low voice, Fischer swore. "I hear someone upstairs—"

Overhead lights flooded the basement. Easton and Ginny stopped dancing. Ginny sensed heat in her cheeks, and she stepped back from Easton. She looked toward the stairs and figured that this was how it would end. An armed burglar or even worse, the cops. A ride to the police station, then her mother driving from Arapahoe in the middle of the night. Bobby waiting in the pickup, covering his mouth to keep from laughing. Screaming. Shouting. A series of accusations. A list of denials. Inevitably, tears.

The man walking down the stairs looked as shocked as Ginny felt. "I was just coming down to get a drink," he said. "I couldn't sleep."

Easton turned to Fischer, nodded, and the tape kept rolling. "We've come to say goodbye."

The man took two more stairs and for the first time appeared to notice Fischer with the camera. The man titled his head to the side and rubbed his jaw. "Did you know my father?" Easton shook his head. Ginny looked toward the door and wondered why they weren't passing through it, back into the night, disappearing like phantoms. "Is there something I can help you with?" the man said.

"I don't think so," Easton said.

"What did you take?" the man asked. He looked around the basement and then back up the stairs, seeming to calculate the distance between various points: the intruders, himself, and the top of the stairs. "Take what you're going to take. I don't want trouble."

Easton locked eyes with the man. "It's nothing like that." Ginny placed her hand on Easton's arm and nudged him toward the door. He shook her off. She wondered what it was that they would haul from the basement. The VCR, the television, liquor?

"I could call the police," the man said.

"You'd have every right to," Easton said. "But I wish you wouldn't."

"No one wants any trouble here," the man said. He seemed confused. He kept one foot still and the other moved up and down between two steps.

Easton took Ginny's hand and turned toward the door. Ginny stood still, staring at the man, her arm bent behind her as Easton walked away. She let go of Easton's hand and began to sing a slow, sad song. "Going to run all night, going to run all day. I bet my money on a bob-tailed nag, somebody bet on the gray." She smiled at the man and waved. He smiled back, his face nearly expressionless, tinted with something between pain and shock.

Fischer stepped back, zooming out to get both Ginny's and Easton's exits as well as the man frozen on the staircase. Once Easton and Ginny were outside, Fischer walked backward, continuing to film the man, who gripped the stair railing as if he were on a ship during a squall. For a moment, the gravity of that imaginary sea seemed ready to pull the man over. Ginny thought she heard him clap, or maybe it was Donald—poor dead Donald—but maybe she only heard the snap of the bolt in the door.

As they walked back to the Affiliate, Ginny stopped in front of an ATM kiosk. She smiled at the camera in Fischer's hands. "The end," she said. "That's a wrap, Fischer. You can go home now." Fischer hesitated and Easton shrugged. The cameraman turned off the camera and said his goodbyes. Ginny pulled a bankcard from her pocket.

"What's that?" Easton said.

"Key to paradise. Keep your face from the camera on the ATM and the one in the corner." Ginny turned her head away from the door and slid the card in the slot. A bolt moved. "Abracadabra."

"Wait." Easton pulled two oversized bandanas from his bag. He tied them cowboy-style across each of their faces. Ginny caught sight of herself in the glass. She removed the bandana, shook it out, and then retied it like a courtesan veil. Inside, they averted their faces from the surveillance cameras.

"I was on TV a number of times as a child." Easton touched her face. "Tragedies, mostly. You know, the stuff on the news. A siege, a shooting, a fire."

"I'm sorry," Ginny said. She hummed "All the Pretty Horses" in his ear. They fell to the floor, tasted each other, left most of their clothes on. They were desperate, they were hungry, and they were quick, but Ginny felt like she would see this for the rest of her life, the re-runs of this love

Several days later, Easton borrowed a car and they drove out to Arapahoe Park. Easton sat at the wheel, Ginny in the passenger seat, and Fischer in the back with the camera rolling. "Do what you need to do," Easton said. He pulled a strand of hair from Ginny's eye. "If you're not back in thirty minutes, I'll assume you're staying." The car windows were rolled down, and she heard the track announcer off in the distance. *We've got a photo finish. Please hold all tickets. Please hold all tickets until our stewards announce the winner.* She knew that if she uttered a word, she would break down into sloppy tears. She kissed him on the cheek. "I'll understand," she heard him say as she closed the car door.

Ginny turned when Bobby walked into the camper, a small TV/VCR showing Easton's hand on her knee and her holding a can of peaches. Ginny and Bobby watched images of the Affiliate, Ginny digging through the garbage, dancing with Easton, sitting in the parking lot at Arapahoe Park. On the television, there were images of people watching television.

"What the hell?" Bobby said. Ginny shrugged and continued packing a small bag. Bobby's face reminded Ginny of the man on the stairs—a composition of confusion and fear.

"Bobby, if you're any kind of brother, you won't tell her where I'm going." They both turned toward the TV.

"She's asked Uncle Charlie to try and find you."

Ginny felt as if it was all rehearsed and she gave Bobby a weak smile. "I love you," she said. "Please?"

When she went to sleep that night, Easton spooned into her—like her own personal ghost image—and spoke into her ear, static she couldn't decipher but which eased her into star-filled dreams.

Maxine Payne

TYRONE JAEGER was born and raised in the Catskill Mountains. He received his PhD from the University of Nebraska–Lincoln and is an Associate Professor of English/Creative Writing at Hendrix College in Conway, Arkansas. He is the author of the cross-genre novella *The Runaway Note*. *So Many True Believers* is his first short story collection. Visit him online at www.tyronejaeger.com.

CPSIA information can be obtained at www.ICGtesting.com
Printed in the USA
LVOW08s0315120416

483119LV00001B/1/P

9 781938 466588